Woman
Under
Construction

Linda G. Hodge

KNOWLEDGE POWER BOOKS

ISBN 978-0-9818790-4-8

Library of Congress Control Number: 2011929603

Edited by Penny Scott

Front and Back Cover Design
Wendy Aguirre – Studio Wende El

Front Cover Photography - Juan Roberts – Creative Lunacy

Interior Design - John Sibley – Rock Solid Productions

For information regarding permission or additional copies, contact the publisher

KNOWLEDGE POWER BOOKS
A Division of Knowledge Power Communications, Inc.
25379 Wayne Mills Place, Suite 131, Valencia, CA 91355
www.knowledgepowerbooks.com

Foreword

Dr. Fred L. Hodge, Jr.

From her humble beginnings in Corpus Christi, Texas, to being the CEO of Living Praise Christian Center in multiple locations in Southern California, Pastor Linda Hodge has a plethora of life experiences to share. She is a wife, mother, grandmother, pastor, author, and the founder of Women of Virtue and Excellence Network (affectionately known as WOVEN). Linda serves as a wonderful example of how God can take a life that is drifting and give it direction and purpose. In this book, she reveals life-transforming principles that brought her to the place of success she holds today.

This book provides powerful tools and practical guidance to help real people, in today's world, to break through whatever barriers they encounter, while reaching for the most fulfilling, prosperous, and authentic life possible. Linda believes that every woman has the potential to win in life; that she should acknowledge and embrace the gift of life as an opportunity to cultivate herself to be the best she can be. The title of this book is indicative of the transformation that will take place in a woman's life through diligence and hard work – no matter what social economic status you hold. By reading <u>Woman Under Construction,</u> you will be inspired to take the limits off yourself and press forward to higher achievements, and fulfilments in life.

It is a truth, that one year from now, your life will change for the better or the worse: It will not stay the same. Why not take this journey with Linda, and build upon the foundations of life God has afforded you? Any effort to implement these principles will produce change for the better. Get ready to advance to your next dimension of womanhood as you embrace each chapter, and know that you are a woman under construction!

Dr. Fred L. Hodge, Jr.
Senior Pastor, Founder,
Living Praise Christian Center

Dedication

To my BEST supporter, coach, and inspiration in life, I would like to dedicate this book to my husband, Dr. Fred L. Hodge, Jr. His unrelenting determination to see the best, and believe the best in me is what has propelled me to undertake such a fulfilling and rewarding project. Thank you, for allowing me to crawl into bed in the wee hours of the night, while trying to complete one more chapter!

To Angela, the anointed scribe and editor, you made me sound like I graduated from Harvard. You are truly the Master Editor. I couldn't imagine writing this book without you.

To my children, and grandchildren, thank you for being part of "Nana's" life! You all have been a part of the construction project in my life. In addition, I am so Godly proud of each one of you; every one of you are a sparkle in my eye!

To all my Living Praise Church Family, thank you for cheering me on and being a voice of affirmation and believing in me.

To Pastor Bridget Hilliard who has taught me that winning is a life-long endeavor that is progressive in its pursuit. Thanks for affirming that life requires overcoming setbacks, and outlasting opposition while realizing worthwhile goals.

To Theresa Kirk, who introduced me to Willa Robinson and the Knowledge Power Books' family! It's the perfect connection that gives me the fuel to sit at my computer and just write.

Preface

We all have visions of what's considered a "dream home." Your palatial haven may be a multi-million-dollar estate in Beverly Hills, featuring an infinity pool, vaulted ceilings, massive bedrooms, and a small putting green. Those seeking solace from city life, can appreciate the 5-acre ranch-style home with its stately, front porch and dramatic brick exterior. Or, maybe you prefer the two-bedroom bungalow with oceanfront views of the Fiji islands.

Well, the house that my husband and I purchased, in my humble opinion, was the cream of the crop. It seemingly surpassed the multitude of requirements we desired in a residence. The laundry list of amenities ran like a scene from the TV show *Lifestyles of the Rich and Famous©*. You could find a spiral staircase leading to vast bedrooms the size of studio apartments. The second-story balconies had breathtaking views. A striking crystal chandelier dangled from the towering ceiling above our formal dining room. Outdoors, you could see a massive pool and spa, as well as a barn for raising chickens. We also had a lighted tennis court, and two garages – one for cars and another for an RV. My husband and I just knew we had purchased the perfect house to spend our twilight years.

However, our extravagant dream home turned into a pathetic money pit with monstrous construction problems. The entire roof needed to be replaced. Through a series of endless power outages, we discovered that our electrical system was an intricate web of wrong wiring set all over the house. Plumbing became a serious crisis. We had backed-up pipes that a "snake" couldn't clear, which led to a disturbing leak from the upstairs master bedroom down to the kitchen. And, when it was really cold one winter, the pipes froze and busted, destroying both garages. What a mess!

While views from the balcony were indeed spectacular, severe water damage on the balcony's foundation prevented us from enjoying the sight. Water leakage also extended to the downstairs' sitting room ceiling. Although our pool and spa offered tranquility, plaster started peeling from the sides and bottom of the pool. So, now we were facing the prospect of fixing the pool as well. Cracks on the tennis court's floor covering called for desperate intervention. To top it off, my pitiful barn became a makeshift morgue – infested with live and dead birds.

I know you may be wondering why in the world I would purchase a home with so many defects. Well, it was a beautiful house filled with stunning potential. There was a magnificent Southern charm. And I, being raised in the South, always had a natural attraction to Colonial-style homes. My abode, in particular, reminded me of a mini-version of the White House. The colossal waterfall in front of the house contributed to the stately charisma. Gigantic multi-colored pillows speckled along the front lounge furnishings helped create a regal ambiance. Our porch was a true veranda, extending across the entire front of the house, where we could easily entertain 50 people. With its enormous doors, the entrance always felt as if I was walking into a palace. Truly, this was a girl's dream home, especially one who loved fluted trim detail. My home was elegance at its finest – if you were a visionary.

Naturalists appreciated the glorious trees surrounding the sprawling two acres. Each season would see new blossoms – a bonus view for any homeowner, and inviting sight for visitors as well. You could hear and see birds chirping in the trees. It was a genuine oasis, where my hubby and I could escape the responsibilities of a busy, but most enjoyable life we shared together. This was a gorgeous home full of enormous potential. But the repair costs far outweighed the long-term value.

Plain and simple: it was *only* a house. A home built by the hands of man. A dwelling erected from cheap, decaying material. And because the foundation of the residence wasn't constructed properly, it could potentially cost an excessive amount of money to repair and reconstruct. Unfortunately, the restoration fees began to prevail over the personal value of the house. We decided we had to readjust the worth of the residence in our hearts *and* mind. Through painstaking deliberation, we chose to lessen the price of the home and made the decision to cut our losses.

Your values, whatever they are, act as a compass, forever guiding you to your ultimate destiny.

This book will equip you with the TOOLS that you need to firm up your foundation. Webster® defines the word **foundation** as being; the basis on which a thing stands, is founded, or is supported; provisions for future maintenance.

The Word of God will be the blueprint as we explore various materials required to ensure a steady, strong and secure foundation. As a *"Woman Under Construction,"* you will be outfitted with the instruments required to examine your life. Every woman, whether married, single, or divorced needs a few minor adjustments here and there. You have only scraped the surface of your potential. Upon completion of this, "woman's life manual to success," you will be inspired to take the limits off your real potential.

A successful life is achieved through continual progression, as well as deliberate and premeditated changes. In order for a house to be maintained, it occasionally needs minor maintenance repairs, due to simple wear and tear, as well as environmental conditions. The reality is that every woman experiences difficult times. Yes, we courageously juggle, while attempting to wear many "hats" through the various seasons of our lives. But, this multi-tasking takes a toll on us emotionally, socially, financially, physically and relationally. Whew! Thankfully, there is help behind these pages.

I would like for you to take an empowering journey with me.

You may have experienced tremendous pain in your life. Possibly, each morning, you already awake to face a few regretful decisions. Maybe, you are gripped by life's disappointments of a failed marriage, or are disappointed in your own career. *This was not how I expected my life to turn out.* Perhaps, you are still living in the past, and unable to see your new and bright future – because you are blinded by your mistakes! *Don't give up.*

The pathway to change happens on the inside! Change is unnoticeable at first to the naked eye. Layers of disorientation have kept your mind in a place of hopelessness and defeat. But, between the covers of this book, you will experience "movement" in your life. I have created a pathway to transformation. Throughout these pages, I will be your "builder" and "coach," carefully cheering you toward the finish line. Stay with me on this road. You are preparing to embark upon a better and hopeful future! Matter of fact, I see your future and it is already looking brighter. Let's proceed to becoming a *"Woman Under Construction."*

Table of Contents

Foreword
Dedication
Preface

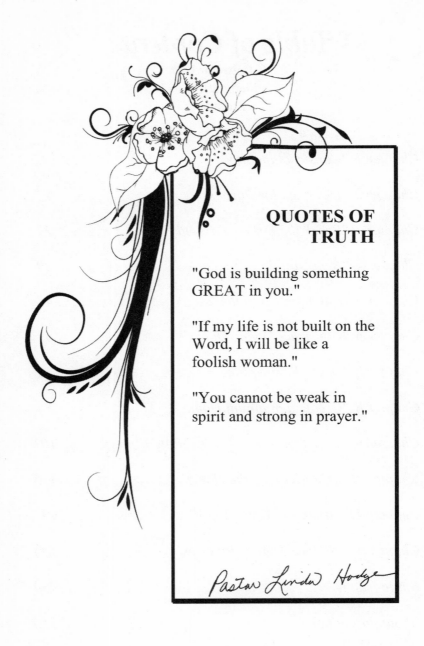

QUOTES OF TRUTH

"God is building something GREAT in you."

"If my life is not built on the Word, I will be like a foolish woman."

"You cannot be weak in spirit and strong in prayer."

Pastor Linda Hodge

Chapter One

Construction Site

A construction site is usually equipped with various tools that carpenters use to assemble, teardown, fortify, and create. Such gear is specifically designed to perform numerous tasks and must be handled with precision in order to receive the maximized benefit of the equipment. These instruments allow handlers the ability to adjust various apparatus parts and complete structures. Certain tools are superior to others, depending upon what's used to produce the final design.

In a scriptural perspective, the woman's role of making life choices is considered pivotal when she's creating her personal habitat. Proverbs 14:1 reads, "Every wise woman buildeth her house." When we build our homes, they should be primed with a durable foundation – strong enough for our homes and families to remain unblemished. Put on your hard hat and create your home or *self* so sturdy that it can endure the blows, storms, and turbulent times of life. This is not an easy endeavor. It takes lots of preparation, self-examination, honesty, and boatloads of perseverance!

God is building something GREAT in you. It's time for you to fight the disenchantment of failure. I have seen a few magic shows and it's amazing how magicians have the ability to create this mind-boggling sense of illusion. Through props and lighting effects, a magician is able to seemingly cut a woman in half, pull a rabbit out of a hat, and make a person levitate above ground. It's all in the trickery of illusion.

In life, there are "props" whose dazzling shows of destructive behavior entice and take many off the right paths. You may be caught in their game and sacrifice a period in your life, while hoping for a return on a failed investment. Eventually, you realize they were *only* illusions – fakes and tricksters, scam artists, or predators. Possibly, for some of you, setbacks in life have caused you to view life from a distorted angle. Maybe, you fell vulnerable to someone, placed all your cards on the table, and thought that surely you had won the hand. Then, you realized that you miscalculated the hand and the player! *Keep going. You will be victorious.*

This new construction site of building your body should be taken with steps carefully ordered by God. More often than not, we want to remodel or upgrade our exterior before we begin working from the inside outward. Despite how much renovation or improvement has already been completed, a sound foundation should be erected first. Foundation is the base that holds the entire structure in place. It is the platform – the root on which everything else is established. Hebrews 6:1 explains, "Therefore let us leave the elementary teachings about Christ and go on to maturity, not laying again the foundation of repentance from dead works and of faith toward God."

As a woman full of unlimited potential, it's time to get firmly rooted in the *right* foundation, which is God. It's your moment to reach for the next level in your anointed destiny. He, alone, knows your self-worth and sees your real capability. Once you've made repentance from dead actions, have faith in God and press forward! *I must be secure in God's love, certain that I am forgiven, chosen, loved and cared for by God.* Know who you are – God's beloved daughter.

[2]

The Blueprint

When you visit a construction site to check out a house or a building that is being created, you will always find blueprints. Can you imagine a carpenter attempting to construct a house without first looking at the drawings? He would be running around in a sea of confusion. The craftsman wouldn't know whether he's supposed to create a Tuscan-, Cape Cod-, or Ranch-style house. When asked what he is building, the frustrated carpenter will most likely shrug then answer, "I have no clue! This is nearly impossible with no direction!" The builder doesn't know whether to place the kitchen in the front or back of the home.

He doesn't know the amount of bedrooms and bathrooms allotted for the area. Without a draft, the carpenter can't readily determine if the dwelling will be made from brick or stubble. Since the designs are missing, the workers aren't sure of the framework desired. The electrical system, insulation and roofing materials remain a mystery. Most importantly, because of the missing blueprint, the builder wouldn't know how much material to use because he wouldn't know the budget set aside for the project.

In life, blueprints are the Word of God. His outline gives us the directions and details we need in order to build sturdy lives. Matthew 7:24-26 reads:

> Therefore whosoever heareth
> these sayings of mine, and
> doeth them, I will liken him
> unto a wise man, which built
> his house upon a rock: And the
> rain descended, and the floods
> came, and the winds blew, and
> beat upon that house; and it
> fell not: for it was founded

upon a rock. And every one
that heareth these sayings of
mine, and doeth them not, shall
be likened unto a foolish man,
which built his house upon the
sand: And the rain descended,
and the floods came, and the
winds blew, and beat upon that
house; and it fell: and great
was the fall of it.

A woman who wants to please the Lord is wise. She will build, by successive additions, a life that is pleasing to God. She diligently constructs a lifestyle whereby her household affairs and relationships bring pleasure and delight to God's heart. My life and yours must be built upon Christ, the *rock*. When my world is raised on anything other than the *rock*, then I don't have stability, staying power or security. Look, I know that as long as I live, the rains of life will descend. It's also true that floods may try to overtake me, and the winds could attempt to blow my hopes. But, at the end of the day, my sanctification will be the guiding force that helps establish my firm foundation.

If my life is not built on the Word, I will be like a foolish woman: When the pressure mounts up and the storms come, I could be filled with negative, despairing thoughts. However, because I *know* the Word, when tribulation and persecution arise, my challenge and victory will be evident. During tough periods, it's very obvious who only *hears* the Word, as opposed to those who *heard* and *practiced* what they learned. It's not enough to hear the Word, you also must understand it.

Let the Scriptures become eternal footprints on your heart by remembering them. Talk about the Word with family and friends. Repeat verses in your daily prayers. Practice it – be doers of the Word. The Scriptures define the term foolish as being rebellious. Consider this biblical concept: The foolish woman tears down her house with her own hands. Thus, a woman can destroy the very things God has given her to build simply because she does not have a clear understanding of her blueprint.

The Frame

The frame is attached to the foundation. We create the framework to determine the distribution of space, or how the space will be used. As a skeleton of the structure, the frame gives purpose on how the house will be shaped and built. If the framework is not built properly, then the walls and all the electricity will not function properly. There will be cracks and defects in the wall.

Our frame is our soul and consists of emotions (feelings), will (actions), imagination, and intellect. James 1:21 reminds us, "Wherefore lay aside all filthiness and superfluity of naughtiness, and receive with meekness the engrafted word, which is able to save your souls." It is not just the Word, but the engrafted or implanted Word. Meaning, this Word must "take root" within your soul because God's extraordinary power can save your soul! Too many souls are cluttered with spiritual debris and emotional junk that's accumulated over the years. *The only way to clean out the clutter is to get real with God.*

Open the door to your heart and allow everything to fall out before the Lord.

Before assembling frames for structures, carpenters quickly inspect pieces to ensure that none of the materials are damaged. This same approach should be taken when building your new human frame. All the contaminated parts must be flushed out! However, God will not violate the self-erected defense you've been using against life's predators.

So, it's best to approach this soul cleansing with a meek and humble attitude. In this way, it's much easier to submit to the Word of God. Unfortunately, the soul man often rejects God's chastisement or *molding* by reacting with anger, hostility, pride, and arrogance. Man's willpower then sides with its own opinions.

Owning a Bible and reading it now and then will not save your soul. Scriptures must become embedded in your soul – have a fixed position to "germinate" or grow into the frame. The Word of God needs to develop from a blade; to an ear; to a full corn. However, it will not blossom in you, unless you have it planted in a fixed position. A plant will never grow properly if it's not placed securely and firmly in soil. No matter how you water it, feed it, or even talk to it, a plant just won't grow.

In order to construct a Godly frame, the spirit and soul must be divided. Only the Word of God can accomplish this intricate assignment. Hebrews 4:12 explains, "The Word of God is quick, and powerful, and sharper than any two-edged sword, piercing even to the dividing asunder of soul and spirit, and of the joints and marrow, and is a discerner of the thoughts and intents of the heart." The Word of God has a way of cutting away and identifying weak foundations and infrastructures in your soul. It is a mirror for the inner man. When you look at the mirror of God's word, you can actually see your inner man. As you read the Bible, you're not only reading it – the Bible is reading you. As I meditate on the Word, which means to ponder, the Word has a way of uprooting poisons hidden deep in the subconscious area of my mind.

Have you ever wondered how you heard a powerful message on Sunday, but could vaguely recall those same powerful quotes by Monday night? There has been a leakage. You don't have to be a plumber to know that certain faucet leaks are slow moving with minor trickles, while other leaks drip quickly in large amounts. Ever mull over why your water bill has escalated when your usage hasn't changed? The larger the leak, the more it costs you. When considering a woman's soul, the longer you allow holes in your soul to exist, the wider they expand. Unhealed hurts, unresolved issues and unmet needs must be identified. Time to fix those holes – once and for all! You've got to know that no amount of money, sex, or food can ever patch up those gaping holes in your heart. *Only God can heal all wounds.*

The Foundation

It is the base on which an object stands, is founded, or is supported; offers provisions for future maintenance. Now let's look closer at the foundation of a structure. I like to compare it with our born-again spirit. Our Christian spirit holds everything together, just like the foundation of a house provides the all-important groundwork for a structure. Using the Christian spirit as a guide, we are able to measure others. We can gauge a person's spiritual prowess and depth in order to determine their spiritual level. The spirit man has the most powerful force in this world. He can size up the thoughts and intents of the heart.

Jesus says in John 6:63, "It is the spirit that quickeneth; the flesh profiteth nothing; the words that I speak unto you, they are spirit and they are life." Jesus explains that the spirit gives life, while the flesh doesn't gain anything. You can be highly intelligent and still go to hell. You can be the cutest thing on the planet and still go to hell. It is the spirit that is the most important. When we truly get the revelation of this, then we put less security in natural talents, charisma, wisdom, or anything else.

Solomon tells us in Proverbs 20:27, "The spirit of man is the candle of the Lord, searching all the inward parts of the belly." What is the Lord looking for? The Spirit of

God wants to use the spirit man to search out the very core of man, the hidden parts. We are told to be adorned by the hidden man of the heart, the spirit man. Through my spirit I learn not to live independently of God, reminding my soul that he has been crucified with Christ. Unless our spiritual experience produces in us a willing acceptance of the whole counsel of God, our spirit is very superficial. I can attend church regularly, but still not be broken. I can pay my tithes and offering and still refuse God's authority. I can even work in the church, and be a leader, but still rebel to the Word of God.

Brokenness removes the hardness, rebellion, resistance, and independence, while producing tenderness, obedience, and submission. In the state of brokenness, you are under the tempering and taming by the Spirit of God. Psalm 51:6 reminds us, "Behold, thou desirest truth in the inward parts: and in the hidden part thou shalt make me to know wisdom." God's Spirit uses mine as a flashlight to reveal and make me known to myself. Your spirit man will not excuse you. He is constantly shining upon you to get you corrected, instructed, and reproved. Your spirit man sometimes has to use *pliers* to remove deadly emotions. They are complex, knee-jerk responses involving physiological changes as a preparation for action. Have you ever abruptly reacted to someone or a situation in such a way that it even surprised you? Then, wondered why you responded in that way. Those are deadly emotions that may try to sabotage you every time.

A lot of people like to paint over flawed walls in their homes. It takes plenty of manual labor and can be extremely time-consuming. First, there's the grueling and meticulous job of scrubbing away old information with sandpaper. Remember, you can't paint it until you repair the flaw. Second, you must cut away the damaged part. Third, prepare the surrounding areas to receive the new piece of plaster, by measuring, cutting and screwing the plaster into the wall.

Fourth, you have to apply the joint compound, let it dry, and then use sandpaper again to even it out. Finally, after the plaster dries, you review your repair work to see if the hole is evenly covered. You may have to repeat the process until the flaw is refinished.

Consider God as the carpenter working to patch up your flaws. Because He is omnipotent, He is also the drywall and plaster. "Living in the spirit," means that I trust the Holy Spirit to do in me what I cannot do myself. This life is completely different from the life I would naturally experience without God. Getting rooted in a firm foundation is not a case of trying but of trusting; not of struggling but of resting in Him. If I have a bad temper, a quick tongue or a critical spirit, then I cannot change myself. Instead, I must seek the Spirit of God to produce in me the needed purity of humility or meekness, and be confident that He will do so. Resting and allowing God to perform His work is what it means to "stand still," and see the salvation of the Lord, which He will work for you (Exodus 14:13).

I know it can be difficult to wait under God's covering, especially when you're single and there's no strong biceps for you to rest upon as you retire for the night. My hat goes off to you. A number of you are courageous, skillful, and resourceful. You are handling a multiplicity of responsibilities, problems and crisis – often all by yourselves. For several women, love is the most important reason for existence. We have been taught early on, that life consists of growing old, getting married, having babies and living life happily ever after.

Our culture teaches us that "romantic" love is a major emotional value, which must be constructed into our lives in order to secure a strong foundation. True, we all need love. But the overly romanticized view of love depicted in romance novels, soap operas and girly flicks is a distortion of true love. Your foundation can't be sought in a "man." No, you can't live your existence through the approval of the male-gender. A woman must first be an individual and establish her own security. Then, if a man does come into her life, she can see this blessing as a bonus. A man should not be the sole reason for a woman's survival. Allow God to be the foundation for which you build your entire world.

The Roof

A roof is defined as the exterior surface, and its supporting structures are located on the top of a building. The term roof can also mean the highest point or limit; to grow, or rise. Despite any savvy techniques used to build a house, a frail roof won't last long. In various poor countries of the world, typical living quarters are extremely flawed because they aren't constructed according to U.S. Building Codes and Standards. Therefore, when countries experience cartographic devastations, their homes and buildings usually collapse. Sadly, thousands of lives are lost when weak structures are hit by torrential winds and rain.

Consider prayer life as your roof. The Bible says to *pray without ceasing*. The phrase sounds like a directive – not an option, but a direct command. And, the simplest meaning of prayer describes it as "talking to God." Prayer has always been an integral part of my life. To say the least, the ability to communicate with the God of the universe is intriguing. Early on in my Christian life, I knew prayer was the vehicle for me to communicate with God. From time to time, my husband jokingly tells the congregation about our adventures of praying in the car together as newlyweds.

I can't count how many times my husband would head down the road, and I suddenly got this nudge to pray. Here I am, fervently praying with the car windows down! Other motorists are driving by gazing in amazement. What is wrong with her? Incidentally, I got a ticket for passionately praying while driving my car home from work. I was so caught up in the moment that the lights on the street were non-existent. Before I realized it, I had run a red light. I reluctantly received my ticket, but learned a powerful lesson. Don't fervently pray while driving. That experience has been a model that I've held to for more than 20 years now. In Philippians 3:10 (AMP), the Apostle Paul says:

> For my determined purpose is
> that I may know Him, that I
> may progressively become
> more deeply and intimately
> acquainted with Him,
> perceiving and recognizing and
> understanding the wonders of
> His Person more strongly and
> more clearly.

Paul's attitude and purpose is the very foundation of vibrant, powerful prayer. It is not just the mouth and mind that prays. Our life is a prayer. If your life is not the eternal, God-kind of life that springs forth from a heartfelt desire to know Jesus, then your prayers will lack force and substance. They will not be, "The effective (heartfelt, continued) prayer of a righteous man (that) avails much," as James 5:16 describes. A solid Christian life (roof) makes tremendous power accessible, and dynamic in its working.

If you're sensing a barrenness in your prayer life, you may need to do as Lamentations 2:19 says and, "Arise (from your bed), cry out in the night, at the beginning of the watches; pour out your heart like water before the face of the Lord." In essence, your soul is like a container that can hold countless things. Most people just try to relate to God from the surface of that container, so their relationship with Him remains very shallow. It's like surface relationships that are insignificant, casual, and have no depth or substance. We all have casual, soulless, seasonal, recreational and petty relationships. But God is after our heart. God doesn't desire a one-night stand, "quick, fix-me" encounter, or a "spare tire" relationship. Nor does He only want to see you when nothing else is working.

Did you know you can keep God out of certain areas of your life by refusing to expose them to Him? You can close the door on Him by failing to honestly communicate. Pouring out your soul is like cleaning out that messy truck. Some things just need to be confessed, put under the blood of Jesus, and thrown away forever. Other things – cares and worries – need to be given to God in faith. The Bible says, "It is impossible to please God without faith." God wants you to bring forth important things in prayer and it requires faith for you to do that.

When we pray, we always travel by faith. Prayer is like a vehicle that takes us from where we are to where we want to go. Every type of prayer requires faith. Whether you're meditating on the prayer of agreement or participating in worship, if you're not releasing faith, then you're not going anywhere. Consider a car that has no fuel. It has the capability to travel down the street and take you to your destination. The automobile has a motor in it, and all the necessary devices to cause it to travel or move. But, without fuel in the tank, the car doesn't have the ability to travel to your destination. Prayer without faith is like a car without gas. Meditation is only empty words that have no power attached to it.

A number of people try to take spiritual shortcuts by simply pulling Scriptures out of the Bible and inserting them in their prayers. Some believers think that just because they've used scriptural words; their prayers will take on supernatural power. I have to admit that I, too, had that experience. I frequently contemplated why my prayers weren't being answered. For the Word to sincerely give power to our prayers, it must take up residence in our hearts.

We must meditate upon it until it becomes revelation from the Holy Spirit and dwells richly within us, (Colossians 3:16).

Once the Word takes root in our hearts, then it is no longer just a bunch of prayers in a leather-bound book. The Word is "alive and full of power...active, operative, energizing, and effective," (Hebrews 4:12). It has become real, spiritual substance. The Words of God "are spirit, and they are life," (John 6:63). They do for your inner man what food does for your outer man. Just as the food you eat supplies energy to your physical body, when you digest the Word of God it provides you with spiritual energy.

While pastoring alongside with my husband for almost 29 years, I've noticed people who feed their spirit constantly with the Word of God. Such believers can more easily follow their hearts. I trust that's because the heart has grown so strong, it exerts a greater pull on them than their flesh. But people who don't feed on the Word have a more difficult time following their heart because it is weak. You cannot be weak in spirit and strong in prayer. No matter how you try to stir them up together they just don't mix.

The popular motto, "Good things come to those who wait," was paraphrased from the Bible. Psalm 27:14 reads, "Wait on the Lord: be of good courage, and he shall strengthen thine heart: wait, I say, on the Lord." Reaching a place where we can consistently hear God's voice calls for an enormous amount of grace, discipline and desire. Waiting on God is the highest and most difficult challenge of the Christian life. But we must pass that test, for it is the key that opens every door.

Yet, knowing this opportunity doesn't deter the difficulty in waiting on God. Why is it so hard for us to listen? Perhaps, the answer lies in the fact that it often takes time for us to hear from Him. It takes an immeasurable ability to wait in His presence. Many find it nearly impossible to quiet their minds and hearts to the static and noise that habitually keep us deaf to His gentle voice. To build the best roof possible, you must Hear God's voice.

I'm so thankful for systematic principle teachings, and we practice that instructional method at each service. We've followed step-by-step formulas as though by systematically pushing scriptural buttons and pulling spiritual levers, we could get Him to produce the results we request. Many of us have even recognized the fact that it takes faith to receive from God. We've studied the Bible, confessed particular verses over and over, and memorized every key to spiritual and financial success. Nonetheless, instead of causing us to flourish in faith and prayer; our endeavors have left us dry, spiritless and occasionally bitter with God. Why is that? It is because we can't have real faith just by knowing principles. Real faith comes from knowing the *person* behind the principles.

Paul understands this in his famous statement of faith in 2 Timothy 1:12, "I know whom I have believed, and am persuaded that he is able to keep that which I have committed unto him against that day." The Apostle didn't say, "I know what I have believed." He didn't say, "I know the principles and steps I have believed." He says, "I know the Person of the Lord Jesus Christ." *Faith and fellowship with God are inseparable!*

Now, as we come to a close of this chapter, "Construction Site," my prayer for you is that you know without a doubt that you are a woman of God. I pray that everything that concerns you will come into divine alignment with the purpose of God for your life. I pray that your spirit and soul will come into agreement. When the spirit and soul are in agreement, then they work together to fulfill the will of God on the Earth for your life.

Hope you have enjoyed your journey through the "Construction Site." Keep your hard hat on we still have more work to accomplish....

Construction Site

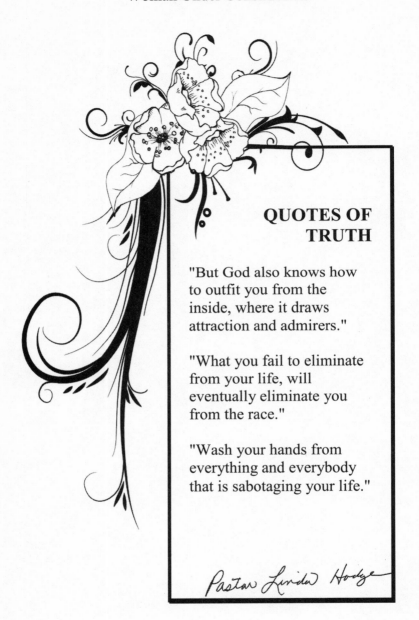

QUOTES OF TRUTH

"But God also knows how to outfit you from the inside, where it draws attraction and admirers."

"What you fail to eliminate from your life, will eventually eliminate you from the race."

"Wash your hands from everything and everybody that is sabotaging your life."

Pastor Linda Hodge

Chapter Two

Designed for Purpose

B efore a designer begins a layout, he or she first must determine the proper use of the object that is being constructed. Without knowing this fundamental information, the designer's labor is in vain. For example, if a dress is being made for a particular woman, the designer needs the client's measurements. A talented designer can look at a person and determine what style would best compliment her figure. If your legs are short, then you would look more flattering in a dress that stops a couple of inches above the knee. But if you have shapely legs, it makes sense to expose the beautiful curvatures of the legs. Ideally, you should never cover up your strong assets. Of course, allow everything exposed according to temperance and modesty.

Fashion designers will also work with you to build upon your current wardrobe. In this way, your revamped closet allows you to appear and feel confident in everything that you do – personally and professionally. The fashion world is a large and lucrative industry, where women are creating their "identity" based on clothes and the designer labels.

Now, here is the dilemma: If I create my identity with the clothes that I wear, where is the real me? The search for identity became an issue during the heyday of the modern Women's Movement of the 1970s. American women entered an identity crisis as they rebelled against the suppressive and oppressive standards our society placed on them. Socially as well as economically, American women were tiring of being treated inferior to men. So, they decided to no longer be strictly associated with the role of mother, homemaker, and John Doe's wife. Women wanted a voice, individuality, and careers – often at the expense of their families.

Our search for significance can't be based on the world's perspective. *As women, our values can only be determined by the Master Designer, Himself.*

A designer by nature is creative. She has the ability to envision a fashion, sketch a pattern, and make the outfit. My mom was a seamstress, and she would make all my holiday dresses. I would love those moments when she was sewing, and getting me fitted for my new dress. Frequently, I would try the dress on to determine if any alterations were needed. After the final modifications were made, I was ready to wear my new dress. I would be smiling from ear-to-ear. I was so proud to put on my mom's new designs. I was unique – special – no one around had my particular clothes. They were made specifically for me.

Our heavenly Father is the world's best designer! When He designed you, He destroyed the mold. He said, "All I need is one of you." Think about it. No one acts, feels or expresses themselves exactly like you. In every sense, you are one of a kind. God thought, "What I'm designing here is rare and special." God didn't create you as an afterthought. Instead, He included you as an integral part of His plan for creation.

Genesis 2:18 reminds us, "It is not good for man to be alone, I will make him a helpmeet." When God looked at Adam, the male human, He knew Adam wasn't complete. God couldn't leave Adam in that state. So He decided to help a brother out. Most likely, He carefully considered, "There ought to be an answer to man's dilemma." After much counsel from Jesus and the Holy Spirit, woman was created. And God said, "This is good."

God is the real designer. Gucci, Prada and St. John are surface designers. They help create the exterior of an individual, whereas God is the stylist of the very purposes of mankind. He knows exactly how to dress you for success. God knows what you need to wear in order to gain favor with men. He is fully aware of what it takes to exist in a world where you are viewed as an inferior in society. But God also knows how to outfit you from the inside, where it draws attraction and admirers. You gain supernatural attention. He will cause people to add to your life and multiply what God is doing for you.

Your design (plan) goes further than how someone views your curvy frame, the classy Diane Von Furstenberg™ clothes you show off, and the red-bottom, 5-inch shoes you painfully strut. It's not about where you were born, the school you attended, or the height of your twin towers. Your plan is what Romans 8:28 states, "And we know that in all things God works for the good of those who love him, who have been called according to His purpose."

A purpose will cause you to; Pursue, Unmoved by others, to Realize your dream. You Push through challenges; Obstacles are conquered, **and** you Soar victoriously like an Eagle = **PURPOSE**

P =Pursue toward the mark
U =Unmoved by others
R =Realize your dream
P =Push through challenges
O =Obstacles are conquered
S =Soar victoriously like an
E =Eagle

When you know that you are designed for a purpose, you have confidence. Certainty is the quality of assurance that leads one to undertake a trial. You possess unquestionable belief that you are able and acceptable. Deep conviction leads one to behave openly bold. A person without confidence is like an airplane sitting on a runway with empty fuel tanks. The plane has been designed to fly. It has been constructed to fly thousands of feet high in the air. Engines have been crafted to carry tons of weight and still glide through the air with seemingly little resistance from outside air forces.

Clearly, the airplane has the ability and potential to fly, but without fuel, it's not getting off the ground. Sure, its purpose is to ascend through the sky, but because one major element is missing, the airplane is grounded. The Master Designer has created you to soar to your destination - your God-given purpose. If you lack confidence, your life will be ruled by fear and filled with torment. When you don't accomplish your purpose, you never know true joy, fulfillment or satisfaction.

We recently purchased a software program for our projection screens at church. The program allows the audience to view Scriptures onscreen, among its other noteworthy functions. However, we were having difficulty getting the program to operate correctly. One of the young ladies went online to seek further help from the manufacturer. She then recommended that the other screen operators in the church's media department also read and become familiar with the FREE software version of the equipment. Why? She knew that the instruction manual is the manufacturer's vision put on paper. Our church member understood that the issues were too advanced for the media department's own resolution. That department also admitted that they did not have all the answers.

The point here is quite simple. Your life and your purpose are exactly like the software program. Problems will occur in life that you don't understand. Our church member consulted the manufacturer of the product to better learn operation applications of our new software. Likewise, you must consult with the Master Designer to truly understand your purpose. The Oxford Dictionary© defines purpose as; a goal, ambition, target, design, and motivation of intent. The Master Designer knows the reason for your existence. Operating as the God-head trinity, He consulted with the tri-part entity about your design and decided with thorough deliberation, on your divine purpose.

Everything you do in this life should be achieved with a purpose. And, people in your inner circle ought to be chosen with careful consideration. It's wise to wear your style of clothes with an objective. Your travel destinations are to be inspired by purpose. Phone numbers you save, and the business cards you collect should all have underlining objectives attached to them.

I recently decided to throw away clothes that were occupying unnecessary space in my garage and bedroom closet. Prior to tossing the items, I meticulously folded and placed them in a secure container. Then, I put that storage bin in a designated area for safekeeping. A lot of the outfits hadn't been worn in years and were outdated. Some were too small, while others were too large. At any rate, those clothes didn't serve purpose in my life any longer. It was time for me to discard those lingering memories of the past. Although our lives have metamorphosed, it's astounding how we find it difficult to release things we know don't serve any purpose. Because your belonging has maximized its objective, hence, it must be replaced or thrown away.

Real contentment is found in the fulfillment of purpose. A person's ultimate joy is realizing that she is *designed* and *living out* her purpose. Such awareness brings a rewarding and electrifying satisfaction. This actualization is significant as well. It puts things into perspective when you know you aren't merely passing through this journey of life.

What you fail to eliminate from your life, will eventually eliminate you from the race. The Bible says,

"You run well, who hindered you?" In other words, who did you allow to subtract from your life and divide you from your God-given purpose and design? Certain people that come across your path aren't worth long-lasting connections. Forbidden relationships usually feed a weakness in you. When Eve connected with the serpent, and was deceived into eating of the forbidden tree, she was instantly disconnected from her Master Designer. Eve's curiosity of the tree and desire to be wise forfeited God's original plan for her.

When God fashions a woman after His design and she lives out her authentic self, He makes her so priceless that nobody can "buy" her. Listen, if a man can purchase you with extravagant gifts or with fancy, empty words, then perhaps you haven't allowed God enough time to process you. What I place around my neck, or carry on my shoulder, does not define me. If you allow someone to buy you with compliments or charm, then you don't understand your Master Designer. You have to examine your relationships, and ask the all-important question. Does this person add or take away from my purpose? Is he always looking at your flaws or complaining about decisions you have made? You may have nurtured a few unhealthy relationships for far too long. It's time to clip the umbilical cord. Those associations have been draining you, feeding off your accomplishments, and depleting your energy. Proverbs 4:25-27 reminds us:

> Let your eyes look straight ahead, and your eyelids look right before you. Ponder the path of your feet, and let all your ways be established. Do not turn to the right or the left; remove your foot from evil.

It's wise to focus and know your intended direction. Keep purpose as your guiding light. Remove all distractions and deadly detours from your pathway. Let's look at a couple of women in the Bible who knew their purpose and refused to give up.

Mary Magdalene lived in a city on the shores of the Lake of Galilee in Jesus' time. She had a face-to-face encounter with Jesus that changed her life. Jesus cast seven evil spirits from her life (see Mark 16:9). After being set free from the spirits that had ruled and ruined her life, Mary Magdalene became a devoted and faithful follower of Jesus. Known as the woman with a messy past, she had many labels attached to her.

Have you ever been labeled or possibly labeled yourself? Maybe, you have called yourself invaluable. Recently during our "Winners' Circle" session, ladies at my church began to reveal how they possessed thoughts of feeling invaluable. It is remarkable how we all look different, come from various walks of life and diverse backgrounds, and yet experience similar feelings of inadequacies. I have heard that a negative thought attached with an emotion can be repeated in a person's mind as many as 600 times a day! It becomes a *dominant thought*. What is constantly dominating your thoughts?

The daughters of Zelophehad in Numbers 27:1-7, refused to lay back and let life rob them of their rightful inheritance. They refused to sit back and accept "wrongs" as part of their purpose. These five sisters lived in the time of Moses and Joshua. Their father died, and the normal custom of the time was for sons to inherit the land of their fathers. And if there was no son, the land was to be divided among other male family members. Daughters were not given an inheritance. Zelophehad's daughters appealed the traditional property-rights custom to Moses, and then to Joshua – and won their case.

Zelophehad's daughters knew their inheritance. They didn't go before Moses and ask for something that wasn't rightfully theirs. The women were requesting what they believed God had promised to them was *their inheritance.* They received their appeal, and not only that, but the law regarding inheritance was changed because of what these daughters of Zelophehad requested, and God confirmed to Moses. According to Numbers 27:8, the Lord said to Moses, "You shall speak to the children of Israel, saying: 'If a man dies and has no son, then you shall cause his inheritance to pass to his daughter.' This word of the Lord became a statute of judgment for all the children of Israel."

Today, most people are driven by excuses and have no tenacity to fight for their possessions. We have a tendency to settle. Every person has an excuse not to work hard or stretch themselves. It takes courage to see a project through the end. You often need guts to step away from the familiar: a challenge can appear risky. God lays before us a test that necessitates us to trust Him, and then act on our faith. The greatest gift you can have is the ability to see beyond where you are now, and view life with the "eyes of faith" – your divine purpose.

Recently, my niece and sister purchased a home. However, it was in need of a few minor esthetics. Drastically worn carpets required replacing. A fresh coat of paint would definitely help brighten the interior of the home. Applying a nice buff to the kitchen's wood floors could restore the original shine. Installing wood floors throughout the remainder of the home would create further warmth and elegance. To top off a more contemporary style to the house, adding new light and plumbing fixtures would make for a lively restoration.

Of course, the renovation didn't take into account all of the new furniture we had planned to place throughout the house. To add charm and sophistication, we considered a new entertainment cabinet to hold the 50-inch flat screen television, as well as statues placed atop the beautiful wood cabinet. The wood mini-blinds throughout the house would form a clean, chic appeal. Lightweight drapes and large artwork spaced throughout the living room would complete the finishing touch. When we conversed about how the house could be transformed to our liking, everyone seemed to envision the renovation. "I love it," I said. My niece echoed, "I can see it." However, my sister replied, "How do you know? You haven't seen it yet."

Here's the irony of the story. It's not what you look at that enables you to be designed for purpose. Instead, it's what you see that determines whether you can walk out your purpose. *The time has come for you to step out of the shadows of your life – and walk into your purpose.* Discover who you are. The moment is now for a monumental shift to take place in your life. Rosa Parks created an epic movement when she refused to surrender her seat, and move to the back of the bus. Unexpectedly, she realized that more was at stake than a ride home. Her relentless attitude caused a light to shine on her that made history.

Now, it's time for you to be raised up. God is saying, "I'm pulling you out of the tomb." John 11:44 says, "And he that was dead came forth, bound hand and foot with grave clothes: and his face was bound about with a napkin. Jesus said unto them. Loose him, and let him go." Lazarus had been dead for four days and was laid in a cave, but Jesus called him forth. The Lord instructed Martha to remove the stone from the front of the cave where Lazarus was buried. Jesus cried with a loud voice, "Lazarus, come forth."

God is calling you forth from the grave. Missed opportunities, and aborted plans are being resurrected again. You are being loosed to pursue your purpose and be all that God has designed for you. It has already been settled in heaven that you are blessed, courageously endowed with gifts, treasures, and priceless jewels. Time to transition from existing to living the abundant life! Wash your hands from everything and everybody that is sabotaging your life. You are designed for purpose!

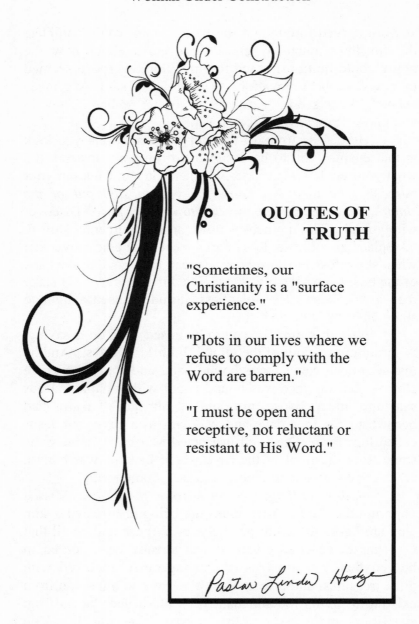

QUOTES OF TRUTH

"Sometimes, our Christianity is a "surface experience."

"Plots in our lives where we refuse to comply with the Word are barren."

"I must be open and receptive, not reluctant or resistant to His Word."

Pastor Linda Hodge

Chapter Three

Break the Fallow Ground

Prior to construction of any type of building or home, the ground must be broken up and prepared for the structure. Various plots of soil around the site of the building must be tested prior to groundbreaking. In most cases, the higher the structure, the more soil testing must be completed. One kind of soil that the Scriptures examine is rocky or stony ground. Even though cleared and cultivated at enormous costs, stony ground often produces only dismal results. This soil is metaphorically compared to man when Ezekiel prophesies to the people of Babylon.

Ezekiel 36:26 states, "A new heart also will I give you, and a new spirit will I put within you: and I will take away the stony heart out of your flesh, and I will give you an heart of flesh." The Prophet was saying here that the stony soil of their souls would be salvaged and made soft and pliable. Through the omnipotent power of God, an incredible transformation would take place in the tough terrain of the Israelites' hard hearts.

Sometimes, our Christianity is a "surface experience." The believer starts off blazing with a passion for the Lord, but slowly the fire begins to come to a quenching, fading light. Initially, when we come into Christianity, our convictions are not always rooted in Christ. Instead, some believers have an unwavering devotion to the church. Essentially, the "church" is considered the pastor, congregation, fellowship, and experience. Believers build reliance upon a sharing, acceptance and concern of God's family. All of these methods are to be commended, and play a part in leading us to Christ.

However, these faith-based experiences are not and can never be used as a substitute for God Himself. Our faith, belief, and trust, if invested only in the church, its people and programs, will lead to disillusionment, discouragement, and despair.

So many of us have the roots of our faith planted in shallow soil. Because of this instability, we are sure to be shaken. Preachers and teachers will, without a doubt, be proven to be less than perfect. When things go wrong, and they will, we will grow hard and cold. Basically, our fire dims because our hope, trust, and confidence were not in Christ. Many choose the *institution* rather than the *entity*. This happens so often, and frankly, no one is exempt.

Let's take a closer look at one of Jesus' parables. Here, he shares an insightful analogy in Matthew 13:3-8.

The Parable of the Sower

And he spake many things
unto them in parables, saying,
"Behold, a sower went forth to
sow; and when he sowed,
some seeds fell by the way
side, and the fowls came and
devoured them up. Some fell
upon stony places, where they
had not much earth: and
forthwith they sprung up,
because they had no deepness
of earth: And when the sun
was up, they were scorched;

> and because they had no root,
> they withered away. And some
> fell among thorns; and the
> thorns sprung up, and choked
> them: But others fell into good
> ground, and brought forth fruit,
> some an hundredfold, some
> sixtyfold and some thirtyfold."

The first analogy God uses here is seeds sowed by the wayside. It was a waste of seeds, and a waste of the gardener's energy to scatter it on such soil. The ground was infertile. Thus, the gardener didn't hope or think a crop would sprout there. That soil was only good for the birds, which were able to quickly spot the seeds lying bare and exposed.

Jesus said some of our lives are similar to that soil. In certain plots, the gardens of our lives have been beaten hard as a rock by people's influences as well as every wind or doctrine we consume as edible spiritual food. We must be extremely careful when allowing others to persuade us. Whomever you permit in your life, you eventually resemble them in some manner. It's incredible how friends begin to sound like each other. They begin to take on one another's dialect and verbiage. The same happens with husband and wives. Couples start to have the same judgment on certain ideas. One person will ultimately persuade the other to share opinions and perceptions.

However, your private thoughts rest in the captain's seat of your life. Bear in mind this popular adage: "I am what I think about when alone – not what I pretend to be in public." This concept strips away the façade and the mask. God's Word in Proverbs 23:7 states, "As he thinketh in his heart, so is he." For those who meditate on harsh thoughts, therein lies hard soil that will not yield to God's transforming power. He does not choose my friends, music, pleasures, desires, or my thoughts. I have the free will to design my own orchestra. *The final choice as to whom or what shall dominate the garden of my life depends on me.*

The second type of rocky ground is what we generally call stony soil. This is land littered with loose stones and boulders varying in size from that of large eggs to random rocks weighing hundreds of pounds. On the other hand, there are areas of stony soil in which the good seeds of God's Word have been dropped. The seeds germinate, flourish briefly, sprout up against rocks of resistance, and then wither away to nothing. In life, stony soil is considered the points and places where a person prefers to disobey God, and follow her own will. This is what it means to have a hard heart! *Plots in our lives where we refuse to comply with the Word are barren.* We block the movement of His Spirit in our affairs, hindering the action of His Word.

This second type of rocky soil is what is known as gravelly ground. It is somewhat fertile land interlaced with layers of pebbles and various loose stones. Seeds or plants that take root here will generally spring up swiftly. Plants will show sudden, spectacular growth, but a few days of hot sun and wind soon wipes them out – they wither away. Such "seeds" speed out of the starting blocks, but halfway around the track, they are out of breath looking for relief. These "plants" slowly fade into the distance and disappear into the world.

The third type of soil, which God refers to as being non-productive, was thorny ground. This land was infested with weeds and thistles. It had the capacity to crowd and choke the grower's plant. God said that some of our lives were just like that. Countless lives are infested with weeds that surround and stifle purpose. God was saying simply that such a garden was *unfruitful.*

Take stock in your own existence. *What is growing in the ground of my life?* Evaluate your soil in another way. *What takes up the most space in my life?*

Jesus made it clear that there were three types of weeds:
1) The cares, anxieties, worries or interests of this world.
2) The deceitfulness of wealth; the attraction of affluence.
3) The covetousness for things; the magnetism of materialism.

Lastly, He speaks about Productive People as being good ground. God was very explicit in describing the spiritual aspect of productive people.

1) They are people who bear His Word and all that it implies.
2) They are people who receive and accept that Word.
3) They are people whose lives, because of that Word, produce the fruit of God's Spirit in their characters, conduct and conversation.

In order to actually hear His Word, I first must recognize it is God who is speaking. Unless His Word is held in great respect as being of divine content, I will simply equate it with other men's words. Then, I must respond to it in a positive way. In other words, I must act on it. If I "partially listen" to God, then the seeds of that Word are snatched away by the birds. I then must run to do what He requests. *I must be open and receptive, not reluctant or resistant to His Word.*

"My son, attend to my words for thine eyes; keep them in the midst of thine heart. For they are life unto those that find them, and health to all their flesh," according to Proverbs 4:20-22. The forces of life that come out of the heart are the powers that change and alter your existence. Examine closely the next verse in Proverbs 4 because the Scriptures are quite clear. Verse 23 goes on, "Keep thy heart with all diligence; for out of it are the issues (forces) of life."

The word, "keep," here means "to preserve or protect one's desires or aspirations, delights, or passions." The reason for *keeping* your heart is that anytime your affections, passions, or desires are divided, you lose the potential of force for change. Religious tradition tries to modify behavior and attitudes without altering your heart, which can only be done through the process of transformation.

A divided heart is one that is competing, uncertain, and is tossed back-and-forth from one decision to another. We all have experienced doubt to some degree; a perplexity concerning a decision we needed to make. You may have written down all the pros and cons to support your reason of making one choice. Then, you list a different reason for making a completely dissimilar decision. Usually, you toss to-and-fro, trying to outweigh the advantages and disadvantages of each option. This is a divided heart. James 1:5-8 further explains:

> If any of you lack wisdom, let
> him ask of God, that giveth to
> all men liberally, and
> upbraideth not; and it shall be
> given him. But let him ask in
> faith, nothing wavering. For he
> that wavereth is like a wave of
> the sea driven with the wind
> and tossed. For let not that man
> think that he shall receive
> anything of the Lord. A
> doubled minded man is
> unstable in all his ways.

If your heart is divided, then you have dual interests, desires and affections. When your heart is split, you will negate the forces that will change your life, as well as the lives of those around you. As a result, you fall out of harmony with the peace and tranquility of God. The moment the soul moves out of agreement with the spirit, you have a divided heart.

The key to releasing my spirit man and bring harmony with my soul is found in the word *brokenness*. We have to break up the fallow ground. Some plots of our hearts have become hardened by exposure to the elements. If you allow your soul to be exposed to the worldly elements for a long period of time, and not open to the things of Jesus, you soul man will begin to harden. It will become rough, inflexible, and non-responsive to the touch of God.

Have you ever attended an explosive service? The Spirit of God was moving, people were experiencing breakthroughs, and many were feeling anticipation and expectation of future advancements. On the other hand, there were a few others present that appeared to be somewhere else. They were completely disconnected from everything that was going on around them. As a matter of fact, those believers gazed at us like we had lost our minds. I don't believe you've experienced genuine brokenness when you can sit in a charismatic service like that, and not be moved with compassion for someone else. What's worse, a few sat there and exhibited attitudes of "when is this going to be over."

You may be in need of a heart check-up; a CAT scan is just what the Doctor has ordered. We have a Great Physician on call here who is a Great Spiritual Surgeon as well. He uses His Holy Stethoscope to hear your heartbeats. If heartbeats are out of sync with the flow of God's Spirit, a problem has been identified. Depending on the severity of your heart issue, The Spiritual Surgeon may repair blockage that has developed over the years. He thoroughly cleans the plate build-up, which has stopped the flow of blood from properly traveling through the arteries. When the arteries are damaged, He places a stint inside the damaged artery. This procedure helps to prevent the artery from collapsing, and thus thwart further impairment from occurring that could be life threatening.

With correlation to the spiritual heart, God actually transplants into your soul a brand new heart that's already fitted with a fresh system of beliefs, attitudes, and patterns of thinking. *A new building is beginning to surface.* In Colossians 3:9-10, Paul was speaking to Christians when he writes of transforming from old ways:

> You're done with that old life. It's like a filthy set of ill-fitting clothes you've stripped off and put in the fire. Now you're dressed in a new wardrobe. Every item of your new way of life is custom-made by the Creator, with his label on it. All of the old fashions are now obsolete. Words like Jewish and non-Jewish, religious and irreligious, insider and outsider; uncivilized and uncouth, slave and free, mean nothing. From now on everyone is defined by Christ, everyone is included in Christ."

In essence, Paul was saying, "Your old life is over." As for you, don't go back into the closet and attempt to put back on those garments – old ways of being and thinking. Those things are out-dated, and never should appear again. He says to put the old ways in the fire, and allow combustible flames to destroy them. The Spiritual Surgeon is operating on you right now. God is giving you a new heart, and everything that has happened before now is of no value. Begin seeing yourself as unique. The <u>Oxford Dictionary</u>©

defines unique as; single, one-of-a-kind, unparalleled, unrivaled, incomparable, unmatched, unexcelled, and second- to-none.

However, I do realize that many women have had their uniqueness damaged, or perverted in some way. I know some have been robbed, hurt and limited in their womanhood. Conducting women's meetings throughout the years, I've recognized the innumerable problems associated with pain – the emotional and physical trauma inflicted upon a woman's sense of uniqueness. Personally, as a victim of emotional and physical abuse in my previous marriage, I can attest to this outlandish treatment!

Sadly, I have heard alarming statistics that here in America, every few seconds, a woman is harmed in some kind of way; beaten, a victim of rape or attempted rape. Such horrendous crimes have become a "devious norm" in our society. Countless women today are now disposable objects at the hands of abusive husbands, fathers, lovers, etc. When a woman's distinctiveness is plundered, it can trigger almost irreparable damage to her and those within her circle. By nature, females are survivors – although they may be beaten, bruised and scarred. Emotional scars are invisible. However, they surface like a tsunami that surges from the bottom of the sea and overtakes dry land.

Thankfully, God has given a system for full restoration of our uniqueness. *Our past does not taint our future*. Many times, our past is a vehicle to get us to our next destination. Every woman needs love and self-esteem to satisfy her sense of uniqueness. When self-worth is limited to the body, and not functioning in totality as a person, tragedy lurks at the door, ready to strike at any moment. The reason why I believe Jesus had a large following of women is because He perfectly satisfied their need for uniqueness. He elevated women to the place that God originally created them to be treated – as joint-heirs with Him according to our Heavenly Father.

Woman of God, you are unique! God created you to be irreplaceable, and where you are impaired, He re-creates that uniqueness in your life through Jesus Christ. Not only are you exceptional, but you are valuable. A woman of value makes her presence known, not by her numerous words, but by her few phrases. She is seasoned with grace and wisdom, and knows what it means to have a ministering mouth. "The lips of the wise spread knowledge...," (Proverbs 15:7). A woman of substance has learned the art of commanding her tongue. When you control your tongue, you can command your life. Numerous lives are out of whack because women can't manage their mouths.

In the Bible, the book of Esther offers plenty of food for fodder. Esther was an orphan, who was raised by her cousin, Mordecai. He was a former prisoner exiled from Jerusalem. She had never known how it felt to live as a free woman in her own land with her people. Yet, she was chosen to be queen over the most powerful and influential kingdom of her time. The King of Persia chose Esther to be his queen. When faced with a crisis, Esther was fearless. She faced the possible annihilation of Jews, and risked her life to petition on their behalf. Esther waited for God's timing and clear direction and then put a plan into action.

"I and my maids will fast as you do," she tells her cousin Mordecai. "When this is done, I will go to the king, even though it is against the law. And if I perish, I perish." Esther stood out from the other 127 virgins who applied for the new queen's position. Esther's value in how she carried herself caused her to excel in recognition. It's time for you to excel! Recognition is awaiting you!

Now is the time to break up the fallow ground of your heart. It's time for soil testing. Time to move, expand, dream again and live! Nevertheless, there is a major difference between "living" and "living a quality life." Mere existence is accepting the status quo and living the ordinary life. But, it's "now time," to move into your full potential.

Eleanor Roosevelt once said, "You must do the thing you think you cannot do." That's a powerful and thought-provoking statement. Mrs. Roosevelt was simply stating, "You have to take a few risks in life to prove that you can achieve your goal."

No more procrastination and no more cop-outs! Get tough with yourself. The human mind, like the human body, has an incredible ability to adjust to gut-wrenching demands. When such strain is steady, regular and consistent, then the result is growth, power, and a greater ease of performance. Make a decision; at least you're moving in some direction. Now, turn the page. You're headed in the right direction.

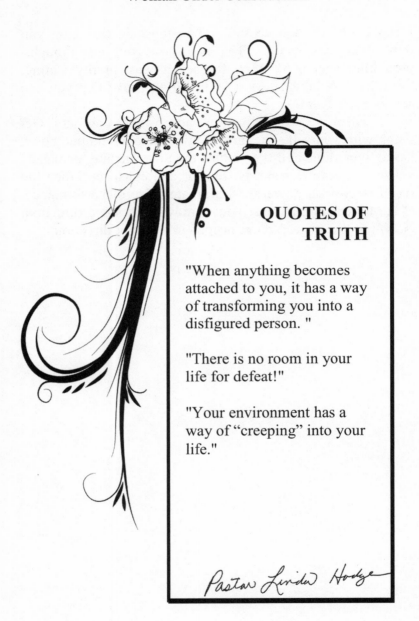

QUOTES OF TRUTH

"When anything becomes attached to you, it has a way of transforming you into a disfigured person. "

"There is no room in your life for defeat!"

"Your environment has a way of "creeping" into your life."

Pastor Linda Hodge

Chapter Four

Bent Nails

My husband and I enjoy visiting model homes in newly-built, planned communities. Recently, we toured several houses that were under construction. Within a few short months, they will transform into beautiful, decorated models for potential buyers. Once a home is completed and ready for viewing, the prospective purchaser will be very observant to look at each room with 20/20 vision. He will pay close attention to the usage of the rooms, size, durability of the home, and if the home fits into his lifestyle.

Despite how striking and dignified the home appears, it alone can rarely bring you joy. You have to envision yourself living there. It's as simple as that. However, as we entered this new construction, the house required a grand imagination to see beyond its present muddled state. The home didn't have any sheetrock nailed to plywood. You could walk throughout the dwelling and find 2'x 4' planks everywhere, but no walls were installed. Nails were scattered along the slabs of cement that we used as walkways. I saw straight and bent nails mixed in the dirt. I discovered still more nails hidden deeper under layers of dust and grime.

Conversely, many of us are buried under iniquity! This "filth" bounds people from head-to-toe and, consists of jealousy, strife, bitterness, idolatry, fornication, and addictions of all sorts. Some of us are buried deeper in sin than others. Thankfully, God looks beyond our mess. He can reach out in time to raise us up – despite the difficulty. God doesn't complain about how deep we're covered, or how crooked we've become. The *hammer* or Word of God can straighten out any bent nail! You are made of the same materials as "new nails" – fresh and right out of the box. God is saying, "I want to use you in my wall."

Your day is upon you. I don't know what you've been through already, but I do know that God is about to pick you up and straighten you out for His Purpose and Design! Certain people may want you to remain a "bent nail," and those accustomed to seeing you in the dirt can't imagine seeing you any other way. Besides, they can't visualize your life as "straightened out." But, if we could hear the re-shaped nails speak they would be saying: "Thank you. The carpenters passed over me, bricklayers walked by me, and plumbers didn't recognize my worth. But God picked me up. Thank you. The cement finishers abused me, and the carpenters discarded me as useless. Oh, how I'm glad God recognized my worth. Thank you!"

Woman of God, your Heavenly Father sees something in you that nobody else can view. He saw something in you that made it worth His time to straighten you out for His Service. His wall can't really be finished until your trophies are placed on it. When God walks through His Church, He acknowledges ALL of the bent nails. I'm sure the devil is telling Him, "Remember what they did?" The accuser of the brethren is working over time, free of charge, to discredit you. The enemy goes back into your history, and reminds God of all your shortcomings, weaknesses and mistakes.

But God responds with His thunderous voice that shakes heaven and hell. He says, "It's under the blood! I don't throw away bent or crooked nails!" God reaches down where you are, picks you up and dusts you off. Then, He uses the hammer of His Word to straighten you out and put you in the hall of faith, as a legacy of hope for others to view as they walk through life's defining moments. *God sees something when man sees nothing.*

When the Prophet Samuel and the family of Jesse only saw David as a shepherd boy, God saw a king (see I Samuel 16:1-13). When God came to Gideon, He said to him, "The LORD is with you, you mighty man of valor!" (Judges 6:12). Gideon said, "Lord is you speaking to me?" The Lord pictured who Gideon was to become in the future, and was not stuck on Gideon's present situation. God always speaks to us in the future tense because He has the forth knowledge of what we are to become.

Consider the life of Mary Magdalene. Jesus knew she was riddled with sin, but He looked beyond her current condition and saw her faith. He cast out seven evil spirits from her life (see Luke 8:2), and Mary Magdalene became a devoted and faithful follower of Jesus. Can you fathom the chaos in her life as she lived with seven demons tormenting her? Do you comprehend the despair that possibly filled Mary Magdalene's life day in and day out? There was no reprieve from the nerve-racking pressure that she encountered.

A relentless, haunting depravity became part of Mary Magdalene's being. Similar to how your hands or feet are intricate parts of your body. You can't fathom waking up in the morning without either one of them. Your hands and feet are the parts of your body that allow you to walk, grasp and physically come in contact with objects and people. Equally, Mary Magdalene's life had become intertwined and attached to sorrow and unyielding failure. When anything becomes attached to you, it has a way of transforming you into a disfigured person.

But the Apostle Paul declares a saving word in 2 Corinthians 5:17. He writes, "Therefore, if anyone is in Christ, he is a new creation; old things have passed away; behold all things have become new." The word, "new" does not mean "new" in time or recent, but denotes "new" as to the form or quality of nature from that which is contrasted as old. In other words, you will be alright because there is a new nature in you! The old lifestyle is no longer the governor of your life. Therefore, since all things have been disposed, the new you has immersed.

To be a "new creation" in Christ means to be made unused, fresh, and unprecedented. Therefore, I now have a fresh way in responding to my experiences; heartaches, disappointments and frustrations. When God looks down upon you, He looks at how to transform your life to help you reach your God-ordained purpose. On the other hand, Satan is overjoyed when we begin to condemn and look down upon ourselves. The enemy knows what can happen when God's women finally grasp the revelation of who they are in Christ.

You have been underestimating yourself.

The great heroes of faith-subdued kingdoms, stopped the mouths of lion, escaped the edge of the sword, and walked through fire. At the same time, we fail to understand that every one of them had the same heartaches, disappointments, frustrations, and temptations as you and I. Before you can rise and march into new spiritual territory, you must be willing to throw off the "chains" of the past. Satan will attempt to hinder you from going forward and obtaining new spiritual victories. He reminds you of the times you failed God. The enemy jogs your memory of all the occasions you've been hurt by other Christians. He will repeat to you all the problems you have faced. And unless you are willing to let go of past hurts, grudges, critical attitudes and fears, you will be forever chained to your bygone days.

There is no room in your life for defeat!

"We are troubled on every side, yet not distressed; we are perplexed, but not in despair; Persecuted, but not forsaken; cast down, but not destroyed," (2 Corinthians 4:8, 9). You may be facing sickness and disease in your body. Or, you are the caregiver of a loved one that lives deals with severe arthritic pain and diabetes. You can face disease and command it to leave, *knowing* you are a daughter of the Most High God. That same powerful life-giving flow of God dwells in you. He is Jehovah Rapha, the LORD, our Healer.

When you are pushed into a corner by mounting financial problems, you don't need to panic or spend sleepless nights worrying how you are going to survive. You can face those financial problems with faith and confidence, KNOWING you are a daughter of the living God! The same powerful force that was in Christ when He multiplied the fish and loaves of bread is in you and will make you victorious! He is Jehovah Jireh, our Provider!

I know you may be thinking, "I feel handicapped by my circumstances which I have no control." And you may be asking yourself, "How did I allow this to happen to me? How did I allow myself to get in this condition?" Well, let's look at the life of a man in the Bible who might have faced tougher challenges than you. My husband was teaching a powerful lesson on Mephibosheth a few weeks ago, and expounded on how Mephibosheth became lame in both of his feet. His nurse dropped him in his early years, which caused his feet to turn inward. Mephibosheth's legs were so severely crooked that he couldn't walk at all (see 2 Sam. 19:26). The accident left him totally dependent on others for the rest of his life.

Mephibosheth lived in a place called *Lodebar,* which means "no pasture." The area around Lodebar was a wilderness that could barely provide food for the livestock or its residences. Often in life, whatever surrounds you develops into your existence. Your environment has a way of "creeping" into your life. Has your environment shaped you? Were you dropped and then abandoned in Lodebar. No worries. God is calling you out of your barren wilderness and your desert (lonely and uncultivated) place.

The Almighty is calling you, who have been abused by the enemy: But God is calling you out of there. You may have experienced significant hurt in your marriage: But God is calling you out of there. Betrayal by your "intimate enemy" once considered a best friend has pierced your heart: But God is calling you out of there. Vulnerability and later "ostracized" has left you untouchable to other trusting relationships. You have converted into a "machine" because machines cannot be hurt: But God is calling you OUT!

Listen! It's your time, and it's your turn to be blessed! Step up and out from the back of the line and take your place! There is no room in your life for defeat because there is a life within you that has never been defeated. There is a life within you that created the universe ... that spoke the sun, moon and stars into existence. There is a life within you that heals the sick, casts out demons and raises the dead. Within you, there is a life that faced Satan, conquered him and destroyed the powers of sin, sickness and death. The same life-giving flow that was in Jesus Christ is in you!

You might have a lot in common with that bent nail that was walked on, and walked over. Perhaps, you were dropped, but now your turn has arrived! And just like those nails, you could have been dropped and kicked around, but those nails had a day of reckoning coming. *God doesn't throw away scraps.* He gathers ALL the fragmented and discarded pieces of seemingly leftover fragments and multiplies them. This is your time of multiplication and increase.

Life is about to change because the Master Builder is bending down to pick you up!

Bent Nails

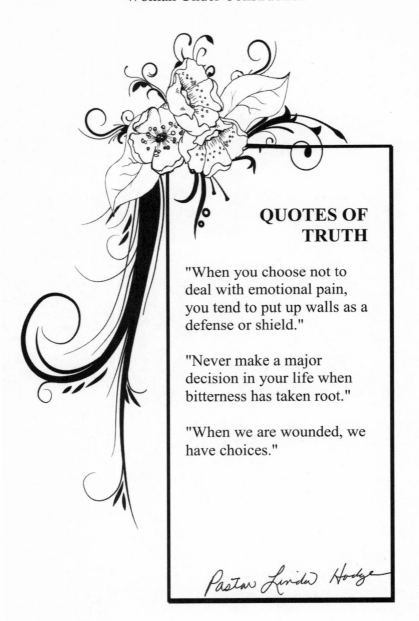

QUOTES OF TRUTH

"When you choose not to deal with emotional pain, you tend to put up walls as a defense or shield."

"Never make a major decision in your life when bitterness has taken root."

"When we are wounded, we have choices."

Pastor Linda Hodge

Chapter Five

Patching Up Walls

M asking is used in construction when building a wall. Sheet rock is placed on a wall, and the cracks are filled in with masking tape. A joint compound made of plaster is then spread over the cracks. This solution helps to smooth out the defects. Once the solution dries, the wall is sanded down. Masking can be defined as covering up. For the purpose of this chapter, we will be exploring "*masking*" as it relates to hiding or concealing our attitudes, hurts, negativity, unhealthy and deadly emotions.

When you choose not to deal with emotional pain, you tend to put up walls as a defense or shield. Walls can help tolerate our own personal injuries. This quasi-security system provides temporary pain relief. Aches are also indicators of emotional or physical discomfort. The fascinating medical series, *Mystery Diagnosis,* which airs on the Oprah Winfrey Network, recently explored what happens when a person doesn't experience physical pain. This particular youngster would have accidents, but walk away ill affected by the injury or fall. After countless trips to the ER and consultations with numerous doctors, a diagnosis was finally made.

Testing determined that the girl was suffering from a rare disorder known as "congenital insensitivity to pain anhidrosis" or (CIPA). The illness affects the nervous system, and the inhibitors in the girl's sensory perception prevents pain signals from connecting to her nervous system.

By not sending messages to the central nervous system, the young girl lost the ability to feel physical pain, as well as sense when her body becomes overheated. In serious cases of overheating, a person who's unable to sweat can go into a febrile seizure. To help regulate her body temperature, the girl must periodically wear a cooling vest for the remainder of her life.

On the other hand, the ability to feel pain can have its advantages as well. Pain sends signals that alert us of impending danger. As humans, we have tried to bandage pain up like the masking tape that covers cracks in the wall. Pain is not a respecter of persons. Its gripping affect takes hold of anyone who will open its doors: Pain can be a silent killer. Both the strongest and the weakest individuals are prone to its attack. Human faculties can't resist the brutal attack on the soul of man.

Let's see how God's power radiates through us in 2 Corinthians 4:6-9 (NLT):

> Let light shine out of darkness, made
> his light shine in our hearts to give us
> the light of the knowledge of the glory
> of God in the face of Christ. But we
> have this treasure in jars of clay to
> show that this all-surpassing power is
> from God and not from us. We are
> hard pressed on every side, but not
> crushed; perplexed, but not in despair;
> persecuted, but not abandoned; struck
> down, but not destroyed.

God's Word shines through the cracks, like beams of light exposing the scared and those in hiding. Unadorned clay pots, vases with cracks. Earthenware jars with chips and dings with flaws. We are people with troubles, perplexities, weaknesses, traumas, and fears. That's all we are without

God. However, with God, we are women with a treasure inside – jewels whose value is beyond price or comprehension. We are women with God's glory at work in us.

When life is hard and God is in us, our broken places don't have to be covered up with man's human limitations. *When life is hard and God is in us,* we who are broken pots can become trophies. Instead of masking your hurts, realize that you can't change what happened. Don't be wounded by your circumstances! The more we focus on the injuries of the past, the more we are victimized by them.

Focus must be practiced before it is mastered. We have to say what the Word says about us, and stop the negative talk. Pessimistic chatter utters thoughts like; "God is punishing me," "I deserve this," "life is unfair," "I hate myself," "nothing ever changes," "I am trapped," and "there is no hope." Such conversation actually reinforces the "victim mentality." They cause us to feel sorry for ourselves and develop a distorted image of reality.

"Let everything you say be good and helpful," Ephesians 4:29, (NLT).

Words have power. Our words matter. *The words we speak to and about ourselves in the silence of our thoughts are especially important.*

Early on in my marriage when things weren't going my way, I would get into this "zone," where I would host a private pity party. No one was invited to this elite party but me and my troubles. I didn't invite outside intruders – they wouldn't understand how I felt. My plight and I had become one voice. No encouraging voices were welcome. I couldn't take the risk of them "crashing" my party and changing the focus.

As time went on and I began to know my authority in Christ, the pity parties became less frequent. Until eventually, those elite festivities became memories of the past. Oh now, don't get me wrong. Once in a blue moon, I'm given an opportunity to be invited to one of those special parties. Nevertheless, I have learned to turn the invitation down!

The Psalmist declares a God whom "heals the broken-hearted, binding up their wounds," adding that, "the LORD'S delight is in those who honor him, and those who put their hope in his unfailing love," (Psalm 147:3, 11, NLT). Although we may believe God is with us, sometimes it's a struggle to sense His presence, particularly when we are feeling low. Pain has a way of blunting our awareness of God's nearness, just when we need that assurance the most. The Bible says, "He is a very help in time of trouble," (Psalm 46:1). In our efforts to cope, we can become so preoccupied with the human realm; what we see, taste, touch, feel, and hear. In essence, we lose sight of the spiritual realm. We forget that the very core of who we are is spiritual.

The Bible says, "The flesh lusteth against the Spirit, and the Spirit against the flesh." This tells us where the real battle takes place. And then it tells us, "Walk by the Spirit, and ye shall not fulfill the lust of the flesh," (Galatians 5:16). If we live in the Spirit, and if we walk by faith, then we can truly "stand aside," while the Spirit gains new victories over the flesh every day.

When Adam and Eve became aware of themselves, their first response was to cover up. They weren't only shielding their private parts, but were also covering up their self-preservation, and self-defense. They used fig leaves as aprons. Irregardless of the clothing we attempt to use as masks over our bodies, we are still naked and open before God. Oftentimes, we try to defend ourselves with excuses. Perhaps, you try to justify your actions and words. Before anyone can be dealt with, we must remove the mask, and all those "fig leaves and aprons."

Years ago, when I was a teenager, there was a popular TV game show that aired called *To Tell the Truth.*

[50]

Two people portrayed imposters, while one individual was "telling the truth." It was interesting because all three characters claim to have the same name as well as profession. They would all answer the same questions. A panel of four celebrities had the difficult task of choosing the right character among the imposters, according to that individual's confidence in responding to the proposed questions. Surprisingly, the "real person" wasn't chosen half the time. Watching the TV show taught me a powerful lesson. It's very easy for imposters to "mask" their true identities – despite the possibility of being effortlessly discovered.

Bitterness

When we mask our emotions, we have a tendency to become bitter. Folks who give up on life become bitter. A prime example is found in the story of Naomi and Ruth. Let me give you a brief synopsis of the story that is found in the book of Ruth.

Ruth was born a Moabite. She married into a Hebrew family that came to Moab from Bethlehem to escape the famine. Naomi was Ruth's mother-in-law. After the husbands of both Naomi and Ruth died, Naomi decided to return to Bethlehem. Ruth refused to be left behind. Ruth tells Naomi, "Your people shall be my people, and your God, my God," (Ruth 1:16). In other words, Ruth says, "My attachment is to you and where you lead I will follow." She went with Naomi to Bethlehem and began a new life.

Unfortunately, Naomi's experiences in Moab had left her bitter. She was angry about the death of her husband and sons (see Ruth 1:20-21). As she arrived in Bethlehem, she was greeted, "Naomi, Naomi!" you are home. She said, "Don't call me Naomi," which means "pleasant." Naomi goes on, "I have changed by name. Call me Mara." This new name means bitter! Don't let life change your name! In biblical times, names were very important; it defined a person's character and their destiny (purpose).

God gave new names to Abram and Sarai. God was, in essence, transforming circumstances in their lives. That's what happens when a woman takes on the last name of her husband. She is taking on his life. The woman's entire identity that was once associated with her maiden name has been changed. When God gave Abram and Sarai new names, God was beginning to speak of "nonexistent things" as though they already existed (Romans 4:17).

Clearly, Naomi was angry about the death of her husband and sons when she chose to rename herself. Obviously, this series of loses overwhelmed Naomi. It can happen to anyone, and everything that happens begins to contaminate your inner emotions. Your heart becomes hardened. The world around you appears problematic. For Naomi, a root of bitterness contaminated her judgment. Never make a major decision in your life when bitterness has taken root. Or else, you will be viewing the situation from a warped position.

Now, let's examine bitterness more in-depth. My husband was teaching on the subject of bitterness, and he has an enlightening definition that I want to share. Bitterness is a self-justified sense of anger that produces feelings, attitudes and actions of retaliation, vindication, non-participation caused by a perceived injustice suffered.

Consider the roots of bitterness:

1. Unforgiveness

When the root of bitterness in Hebrews 12:15 gets a foothold, the first thing that happens is a record of wrongs. The Scripture reads, "Looking diligently lest any man fail of the grace of God; lest any roots of bitterness springing up trouble you, and thereby many be defiled." A root can be defined as; a base, foundation, source, seat, cause, or origin of an object. In order for a root to be removed, it has to be uprooted, eradicated, eliminated, destroyed, exterminated, or uncovered. You must dig it up, and bring it to light. Those are all "action" words that describe how to handle roots. The terms aren't passive or carefree.

How many of you are still having flashbacks about offenses made against you? If I mention, Aunt Rosie's name, you'd probably be able to give me 15 reasons why you don't like her. And not to mention that ex-husband of yours who took you to the "cleaners and back," both emotionally and financially. Let's not forget your first embarrassing moment when your first-grade teacher put you on total blast, in front of the whole class. You're still crawling your way from under that "thrown under the bus" experience!

2. Resentment

Resentment is the record of wrongs now being fueled by lingering feelings, where you frequently meditate and chew on negative emotions. It is astounding to me that when we have feelings of resentment, we think about Aunt Rosie up here (in our mind), but we feel her down here (in our heart). Why is that? Your mind hosts your soul. But your spirit lives in your heart. You are a spirit being: You have a soul, and you live in your body.

Resentment is a spiritual problem, not a psychological problem. Bitterness, unforgiveness and resentment are all spiritual problems, not psychological dilemmas.

3. Retaliation

After resentment gets a foothold, then we have retaliation. Once dislike has started to simmer, we find ways to get back at the person who created those emotions. Retaliation wants to make the person pay. Remember the adage, "I just can't let him or her get away with this? I have to do something!" We spend the rest of our lives trying to get even.

4. Anger

Soon after retaliation plants its grip, then anger comes through the open doorways. Unforgiveness, resentment, and retaliation have been brewing and now real strong feelings of anger appear.

5. Hatred

Hatred quickly follows anger. Abhorrence says, "Because I'm remembering what you did to me, because I have been meditating on it and I really resent it, I'm going to get even!" This emotion justifies itself saying, "I'm turning up the heat. You don't have any reason to exist anymore, especially in my mind and in my presence." Hatred says, "There's not enough room on this planet for you and me at the same place, nor at the same time. Eventually, this emotion develops into elimination modality.

6. Violence

Violence trails behind hatred. This destructive behavior says, "Before I eliminate you, you're going to feel my pain. You're going to hear my voice; you're going to know my hatred; you're going to experience what I feel."

7. Murder

Once violence erupts, the final fruit of bitterness is murder. This can be actual physical murder, or murder with the tongue, which is character assassination or verbal abuse. When hatred, violence and murder are in someone's life, the person feels justified and that everybody else will pay the price. Have you been a victim of this? Did you feel defiled?

Bitterness is a slow lingering procession, and each of the seven areas progressively becomes worse than the one preceding it.

How to Overcome Bitterness:

1. Acknowledge you are experiencing bitterness.
2. Repent to God for allowing you to be in bitterness.
3. Forgive your offender and his offenses against you.
4. Renounce satanic triggers and doors – give him no place.
5. Walk by faith when forgiving the offender.
6. When you repent, receive forgiveness by faith.
7. Use your mouth for positive communication and edification.

Look yourself in the mirror and say:

I am not a product of my past experiences.
I am not a product of my environment.
I am not who other people say that I am.
I am who God says I am.
I am who God is calling me to be.
I am releasing the pause button from off my life.

"The LORD is close to the brokenhearted; he rescues those who are crushed in spirit," (Psalm 34:18, NLT).

God has resources to meet our needs that can only be accessed in and through His Spirit. But we must tap into His supply line. When we are wounded, we have choices. We can obsessively look within and be consumed by our conflicts, or we can cry out to God. You can ask Him to embrace you with His healing presence, and be who you need Him to be in the moment.

God knows our frailties and how life's blows can nearly knock the breath out of us. He sees when our world is completely shattered. God also senses when we're so overwhelmed that we don't even know to how to pray. Sometimes, all you can do is muster up the word, HELP! The Almighty then throws His lifeline to you and pulls you out of despair. Depending on your resistance to the pull from the pit, determines how long it takes to experience the dawning of a new day. This is where the light of hope and restoration is revealed.

David, who endured some dreadful wounds of his own, speaks of God's faithfulness to hear and respond:

> My heart is in anguish. The
> terror of death overpowers me.
> Fear and trembling overwhelm
> me. I can't stop shaking… But
> I will call on God, and the
> Lord will rescue me. Morning,
> noon, and night I plead aloud
> in my distress, and the LORD
> hears my voice. He rescues me
> and keeps me safe from the
> battle waged against me, even
> though many still oppose me…

> Give your burdens to the
> LORD and he will take care of
> you, (Psalm 55:4-5, 16-18, 22,
> NLT).

It's time to "Unmask the Walls." Take off the pretentious mask, and wash off the under-eye concealer that is covering up the dark circles under your eyes. Remove the foundation that is hiding your blemishes. Wash off the pressed make-up powder from your face, which is masking your color tone imperfections. Strip off the false eyelashes and wipe away your lipstick. Let God see the REAL you! It's time to move on!

As Benjamin Franklin once said, "The things which hurt, instruct." Hurts and difficulties are possibly the very best experiences we can have.

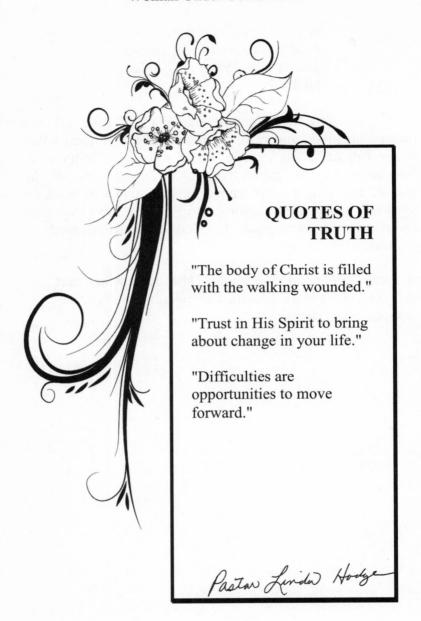

QUOTES OF TRUTH

"The body of Christ is filled with the walking wounded."

"Trust in His Spirit to bring about change in your life."

"Difficulties are opportunities to move forward."

Pastor Linda Hodge

Chapter Six

Construct Divine Doors

For many homes, the front door creates a defining first impression. Sure, its main goal is to offer an entrance and exit for your home, but a door also offers a glance of the home's main design. As I mentioned earlier, my dream home had the towering double doors that were reminiscent of the White House. They were white and made of solid wood. The double doors' frames and trims had elegant, extremely regal flair designs. Every time I walked through those doors, I felt like I was entering a palace.

Let's look for a moment at energy-efficient front doors. It's extremely important to use exterior doors made of heavy, solid wood, metal or fiberglass. The typical, hollow bedroom doors won't stand up to the harsh weather and environmental beatings that front doors experience over the years. Weather stripping around the door's perimeter ensures a tight seal, while caulking around the door's frame helps prevent drafts and keep the warm weather indoors during the winter. A door sweep also stops air from escaping or entering under the door.

When you consider the spiritual ramifications of safeguarding our bodies, it's imperative that we take that same aggressive approach to blocking the most powerful demonic forces. Conversely, in life, Spiritual Doors of access allow entrance for demonic spirits to enter our souls. Doors originate from; bitterness, unforgiveness, anger, jealousy and the list goes on. Wherever there is vulnerability or sin in any area of your life, there lies the opportunity for a spiritual door to open. The enemy is constantly checking you out from every angle to see if you are impenetrable in your stand for righteousness.

If you look beyond the façade and plastered smiles on the Sunday morning faces, you will find that the body of Christ is filled with the walking wounded.

Spiritual Doors

In order to learn more about spiritual doors, we first must define the meaning of "door." It is a passageway for entrance or exit out of a place. Doors offer access or give admission into a destination. They are also portals of entry for buildings. In the Bible, we are listed as a sort of edifice that has portals of entry. I Corinthians 6:19-20 says:

> What know ye not that your body is the temple of the Holy Ghost which is in you, which ye have of God, and ye are not your own. For ye are bought with a price: thereby glorify God in your body, and in your spirit, which are God's.

1 Corinthians 3:10 reads, "For we are laborers together with God; ye are God's husbandry, ye are God's building." The analogy is that we must look at our bodies as temples – houses of the Lord and God's building. A house has windows and doors. For a person to gain access to the interior of a house he must come through the door. There are doors in the spirit just like there are doors in the natural house. In order to determine who has the right of passage, we

must look at the Creator for order. God, Himself, sets the rules for passage and entry.

The Rule for Doors is set by God, Himself

According to Revelation 3:20, "Behold I stand at the door, and knock: if any man hears my voice, and opens the door, I will come in to him, and will sup with him, and he with me." Now, let's examine the rules God has decreed:

1. There must be Exposure to something – I stand at the door means I have come for you.
2. Not by domination but by invitation – there is a knocking and beckoning.
3. Hear my voice – speaks of comfort and familiarity – be careful of hearing strangers' voices. Too often it gets familiar and you get common with it, then you are prone to take the next step.
4. You must open the door – the familiar voice gives you a sense of safety and trust, so you open the door to the voice and let the visitor in.
5. I will come into him – when you open the door the visitor enters and gains access to other rooms.
6. The visitor will sup (eat the evening meal) and have covenant with you.
7. He with me – you begin to enjoy, welcome and pursue the fellowship, his presence has become addictive. You like it so much, you want the visitor to stay and make his abode there (your heart).

A Visitor Can Only Enter By Permission

If God will not violate our will, He certainly won't allow the enemy to do the same, or any human being as well. For someone to get into your house, they must be invited. It can be extremely upsetting for an individual to enter your dwelling uninvited. The door must be opened from the inside voluntarily. The intruder or the visitor must be given permission. The rule applies to humans, spirits, and angels. Even Satan, himself, must be given permission before entry. 1 Peter 5:8-9 remind us:

> Be sober, be vigilant; because
> your adversary the devil, as a
> roaring lion, walketh about,
> seeking whom he may devour.
> Whom resist steadfast in the
> faith, knowing that the same
> afflictions are accomplished in
> your brethren that are in the
> world.

Some believers think they are cursed or trapped unsuspectingly without a cause. They are taken by total surprise when something negative arises in their life bringing troubling consequences with it. Nothing happens without reason. Consider what Proverbs 26:2 says, "As the bird by wandering, as the swallow by flying, so the curse causeless shall not come." This Scripture is stating that actions don't occur without provocation.

Access Doors of Addictions

Our churches are filled with struggling saints – simply trying to survive. Daily, our families, finances, homes and hopes are being shattered and dismantled. Statistics show alarming rates of divorces, suicides, and murders. And what's worse, the rapid rate of prescription- and street drug abuse are at all-time high proportions. Let's not forget the new drug of choice, "pornography" also known as "porn," is continually escalating among both men and women. I recently had a startling telephone conversation with a friend who informed me that porn is more addictive than drugs. It's a billion-dollar entertainment industry, that's accessible for even children over the Internet.

This society has become "addictive-driven." The dictionary's definition of addiction is quite general; "applying or devoting oneself habitually." So, we can say a person can be considered addicted, when they; display an "overpowering, repetitive, excessive need for some substance, object, feeling, act or personal interaction." However, addiction takes on a more thought-provoking meaning, when you consider how it can access our spirits.

Addictions serve as a scapegoat with a primary purpose of steering us from our true feelings. This irrational craving offers a getaway – form of escape. It serves the function of helping us avoid the real anxieties of life by disengaging from reality. Eventually, the compulsive urges to escape take control of the addict, transcending all logic or reason. My husband and I have spoken with countless drug addicts, and the common thread among them all is that the urge is extremely strong. Most addicts genuinely enjoy the rush and have formed a relationship with the substance, alcohol, sex or whatever the choice of drug.

The "habit" always involves pleasure. Ironically, it eventually harms or destroys the body and the mind.

[63]

Unfortunately, it also damages relationships, and devastates loved ones. I have sat across the couch from addicts numerous times to hear, "But I love my spouse! I want my marriage! I just can't quit!" Addiction can steal your life from under your very nose, while you stand there with your mouth wide open.

Access Doors of Shame

When past failures, and dissatisfaction looms to an all-time high, shame enters. Too often, our self-image rests solely on an evaluation of our past behavior, being measured only through memories. Can you imagine buying stock based on the references of a consumer who purchased the same stock five years ago? Society has dramatically changed within the last several years. Yet, day after day, year after year, people build their future and hopes upon the rubble of yesterday's failures.

Much of today's decisions are being made based on actions of the past. Why? Some haven't pulled their thoughts out of the past's pile of garbage. By the grace of God we can change! We can persevere and overcome! *Any change in our behavior, requires us to close the door.* You must be released from your old self-concept, which was founded in failure. To accomplish this, you must base your self-worth on God's opinion of you. Trust in His Spirit to bring about change in your life.

By definition, shame is a deep sense of inferiority. Feelings of inadequacy can destroy your self-worth. It has been proven that we behave in a manner that is consistent with our perception of ourselves. If I can change my perception of myself, I can change my behavior. And, if I can change my behavior, I will ultimately change the course of my life. You are not in subjection to your past: Your past has only been a *temporary* detour to your future.

Occasionally, when driving, I run into a sign that says, "Detour." A detour is only an alternate means to reach my appointed destination. The detour may take me a little out of the way or a bit longer to get back to my final purpose or aim. But, if I follow the detour sign correctly, trust the instructions, and be patient, I will get there.

Woman of God, you may have had some detours in life that has caused some shame issues. But that's OK! "So after you have suffered a little while, he will restore, support, and strengthen you, and he will place you on a firm foundation," (1 Peter 5:10, NLT).

The Approval Trap Door

Several people establish their self-worth on what they believe others think about them. The need for approval causes us to constantly strive to please others, even at the expense of ourselves. If they say, "run," we respond, "how fast," or if they say, "jump," we ask, "how high." Have you ever felt like a vending machine? It feels like an invisible lever is pulling on your body, and you are dropping out whatever is requested – free of charge. Eventually, deep resentment emerges.

The world we live in is filled with people demanding that we please them in exchange for their approval and acceptance. We have become controlled and snared by their subtle ways. Numerous teenagers have admitted to experimenting with drugs or sex due to a need to belong. Just think about it. Compromising your belief based on false acceptance runs the risk of developing a destructive habit that can alter your life forever. Think about Romans 12:2, (NLT):

Don't let the world around you
squeeze you into its own mold,
but let God remold your minds
from within, so that you may
prove in practice that the plan
of God for you is good, meets
all His demands, and moves
toward the goal of true
maturity.

The need for approval boils down to the fear of
rejection. This negative response is actually a form of
communication. It informs another individual how little we
respect him. Rejection may come in the type of an outburst,
anger, a disgusted look, an impatient answer, or a separation.
Denial can be so subtle and destructive at the same time.
Without laying a hand on anyone, we can send the message
that our targeted individual doesn't measure up. We are left
feeling denounced, devalued, and devastated.

However, rejection is only effective as long as we
keep people at a comfortable space, where we hope to
control our emotions. For family members, "I can love you
from a distance." But you don't have to be in my "circle of
love." I choose to put you in a safe place in my life. Fear of
rejection exists only because we base our self-worth on the
opinions of others, rather than on our relationship with God.
Depending on others for value brings bondage, while abiding
in the truths of Christ's love and acceptance brings freedom
and joy.

In Galatians 1:10, Paul clearly draws the line
concerning approval. He says, "For am I now seeking the
favor men or of God? Or am I striving to please men? If I
were still trying to please men, I would not be a bondservant
of Christ." According to this Scripture, we can seek either
the approval of men or the approval of God as the basis of
our self-worth. We cannot seek both. Therefore, the only

way we can overcome rejection is to value the constant approval of God over the conditional approval of people!

Unlock the Door of Unforgiveness

"And be ye kind one to another, tenderhearted, forgiving one another, even as God for Christ's sake hath forgiven you," (Ephesians 4:32).

We will receive God's forgiveness in exactly the same manner that we offer forgiveness to others. In times of trouble and pain, enduring offenses and attempting to forgive are not easy challenges. But we can find safety and assurance. "We can glory in tribulations also: knowing that tribulation worketh patience; and patience, experience; and experience, hope," (Romans 5:3-4). The Greek definition for experience means acceptable, proven, tried, trusted, and tested. In other words, experience is character that has been proven.

Untried, untested, intemperate faith is not overcoming faith, it is baby faith. Infants do not understand the purpose of their faith. Belief is not given so you can avoid the hard times: It is deposited to assist you through the hard times. Every time you come out on the right end of a trial, full of faith and forgiveness, you become refined like gold.

Our Struggle with Forgiveness

Webster's Dictionary© defines forgiving as; ceasing to feel resentment against an offender. Forgiveness must be a conscious act of the will to deliberately pardon another individual, period. It doesn't matter whether or not your feelings have ceased. Nor does it depend on whether or not

God intends to judge the offender. You must still forgive the wrongdoer.

Soon after my husband concluded his mid-week Bible study series on "Regret," a question came up regarding forgiveness. In essence, the question was posed, "What if I choose peaceful co-existence? Can I just ignore him or her?" This is an excellent question because it describes how many of us feel about forgiveness. Some of us become passive-aggressive in our attitude. Lots of believers are excellent at this passive method of dealing with unforgiveness.

You may convince yourself that you have forgiven this person and simply don't feel the same connection. But how do you know if you have pardoned that person? If you still have that ugly, hurtful, painful memory of how the offender harmed you – then you have not shut the door on unforgiveness. True forgiveness has a way of reducing a bad memory to nothing more than a fact of your past with no power to produce flashbacks.

In the parable of the two debtors (in Matthew 18:23-35), the debt the king forgave was enormous compared to a small debt owed by another to the affluent man who had just been forgiven. Yet, that rich forgiven man went right out and demanded a poor servant instantly repay a tiny debt to him. The man had been forgiven of so much by the king, yet he refused to extend forgiveness for a servant's small debt to him. This unforgiveness cost the affluent man everything. He lost the forgiveness of the king and was sentenced to jail, and to be turned over to the tormentors. If we don't forgive, we can be turned over to the tormentors. The original Greek word for tormentors is torturer; one who brings pain; torment; one who harasses and distresses; and one who tosses and vexes with grievous pain of body or mind. We know these names as; depression, fear, anxiety, disease, to list a few.

Nothing Can Replace Forgiveness

You can repent of your sins until you are hoarse; pray without ceasing; pay tithes and offerings; read the Bible three times a day; and still block God's forgiveness with an unforgiving heart! None of the above will cover unforgiveness! Real forgiveness is not cheap. It carries a very high price tag. You must and you can forgive!

Fasten the Door of Regret

As I've mentioned earlier, the Bible has definite instructions on how to prevent our bodies from opening spiritual doors. None the less, because regret is such an overpowering emotion, it's worth exploring further. We must approach regret with the same relentless motivation as if we are weather-stripping our homes – create a tight seal so no spirit can enter. Consider Philippians 3:13:

> Brethren, I count not myself to
> have apprehended: but this one
> thing I do, forgetting those
> things which are behind, and
> reaching forth unto those
> things which are before, I press
> toward the mark for the prize
> of the high calling of God in
> Christ Jesus. Let us
> therefore, as many as be
> perfect, be thus minded: and if
> in anything ye be otherwise
> minded. God shall reveal even
> this unto you. Nevertheless,
> whereto we have already

attained, let us walk by the
same rule, and let us mind the
same thing. Brethren, be
followers together of me, and
mark them which walk so as
ye have us for an example.

Let's define the word "regret," which means to feel sorry, disappointed, or distressed. To remember something with a feeling of loss or sorrow; to mourn, a feeling of distress or disappointment about something one which could be different based on circumstances. Regret is very impulsive, which is to act on impulse rather than thought; a sudden wish or urge that prompts an unpremeditated act of feeling; an abrupt inclination. It is also a motivating force or tendency. Regret sometimes comes camouflaged. It will come in the form of;

Anger – With this emotion you brood over past hurts that aren't resolved and held onto for long periods of time for self-pacification.

Sadness – The memory of an action, decision, or experience that throws you into deep unhappiness, negative meditation or a grieving state. The continuous relapse into this state of sadness will produce depression.

Shame – A painful emotion caused by a strong sense of guilt, embarrassment, unworthiness or disgrace.

Condemnation – To express strong disapproval for an action; pronounce judgment against; and sentence an individual. To judge or declare to be unfit for use or consumption usually by an official order.

Unworthiness – This means insufficient worth; undeserving; lacking value or merit; worthless. It can be a negative emotion that hinders and blocks a person's progress; a refusal to permit or allow one to advance, elevate or enjoy the results of either because of feelings of non-entitlement.

Inflamed memory – Repetitious thought that consumes the mind concerning bad choices that leads to long-term negative consequences.

Missed opportunities – Possibilities that were put before you, like promotions, advancement, and elevations you could not see because of the blindness of regret or bitterness. Regret in this area of missed opportunity also can be the product of the lack of courage to pursue. You were given the opportunity, but didn't have the motivation, courage, or passion to pursue it.

The Dynamic Affects of Regret on Your Life

Regret has a way of pulling and holding you back. It actually causes you to have fear, where you are paralyzed and unable to move. Its counter partner is distraction. The continual lingering memory of the past is a distraction, keeping you from reaching forward. The cousin of regret is bitterness: It loves to blind you to what's possible for your life. Regret always keeps you facing backwards. Unfortunately, living in your historic past will drive you into the cul-de-sac of emotional pain, loss of time, and life.

Regret starts with a bad experience, that transitions into self-punishment. Satan the accuser shoots fiery darts into your head. His direct aim keeps you in condemnation and shame.

Breakthrough a Life of Regret:

Step 1: Renounce mental replays.

Erase images associated with the bad memory: They sustain and fuel it. "Casting down every imagination and everything that exalt itself against the knowledge of God, and bring every thought captive to the obedience of Jesus Christ," (2 Corinthians 10:5). You don't have to live at the mercy of the images that try to keep you chained to your past. Ask the LORD to remove the thoughts from your mind!

Step 2: Talk it out

Find someone you can trust. You should have seven people in your life that will encourage you and tell you the truth. Make yourself accountable to them and speak with them regularly. Talking it out has a way of bringing understanding. When you talk about it – the issue no longer holds you captive. When truth is revealed, lies are exposed.

Step 3: Remind yourself that forgiveness is necessary for your freedom

The amazing thing is that when we come to God, confess our sins, and ask for forgiveness… He forgives us. The Bible says it clearly: "If we confess our sins to him, he is faithful and just to forgive us and to cleanse us from every wrong," (1 John 1:9, NLT). He wants us to forgive others – and not because they deserve it. Nevertheless, He asks us to forgive them because He forgave us first. Accepting God's forgiveness and forgiving others are both necessary in order to experience full and complete healing.

Step 4: Put the Past behind You

There are no such things as "forgiving and forgetting." Let's face it. Once memories are logged in our mental computer, they are there for life. Thankfully, "forgetting" is not a prerequisite for healing our wounds – nor is it necessary for forgiveness. What is necessary is that we face the facts of our wounds, relinquish replays and revenge.

Step 5: Confess the Word of God

Through the years I've strengthened my faith by my confession:

When your **feelings** say, "God has left me, He doesn't care. You're on your own. . ." . . **Faith says**, "In God's kingdom everything is based on promise, not on feeling."

When your **feelings** say, "People will rip you off. Don't trust them"...**Faith says**, "God is my Redeemer. He will return whatever is stolen, one way or another."

When your **feelings** say, "You're going to be on hold forever"...**Faith says**, "My time is in God's hands. His plans for me will be accomplished right on schedule."

When your **feelings** say, "You can't trust God. Look how He has let you down"...**Faith says**, "God has proven His trustworthiness by sending His Son to die on the cross for me."

Difficulties are opportunities to move forward. They will either bring out the best or the worst in us, depending on how we see the opportunities. Troubles transform us, if we let them. Challenges are empowering and can take us to the next level. Are you up for the challenge to go to your next elevation?

Let's Shut the Doors, "I hear them closing now" it's time to move forward!

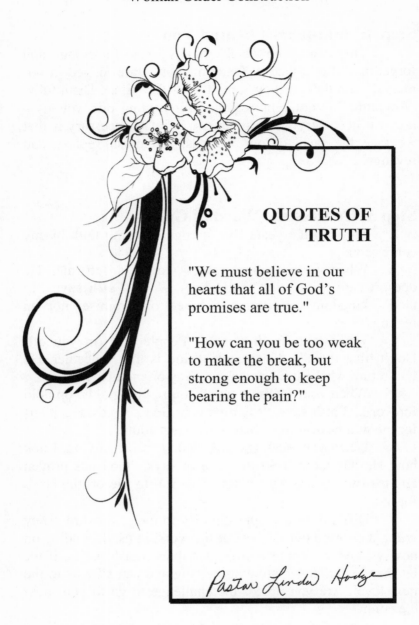

QUOTES OF TRUTH

"We must believe in our hearts that all of God's promises are true."

"How can you be too weak to make the break, but strong enough to keep bearing the pain?"

Pastor Linda Hodge

Chapter Seven

Home Renovation

R enovation is defined as; to bring something such as a building back to a former better state by means of repairs, or remodeling. It also means to give new vigor to somebody or something. Oftentimes, renovating a house is a dirty, tedious and inconvenient job to say the least. I enjoy watching *HGTV©*, and when a home or room is being remodeled, it always appears to be a mass of confusion during the process. The demolition team is hammering away on the already existing structure. Sometimes more pressure is needed, depending on how tight the attachment is embedded into the frame or foundation. There are nails and screws that have to be forcefully pulled out, sheetrock must be torn from the wall, and plaster must be disconnected.

If these objects could talk I'm sure they would be hollering, from high A to G flat saying, "Leave me alone! I've been attached to my source for far too long! Now you've decided after all these years that you want to dismantle me, and replace me with something new!"

Tireless days are spent trying to meet deadlines. Attitudes are flying; co-workers are irritated for the smallest reasons. Renovation teams are aching, from the demanding labor of continual force striking in the same direction and motion. Mental fatigue has set in, where days of the week have effortlessly rolled into one another. By now, the construction crew is thinking, "We've got to get this job done."

The story above describes what many of us contend with when we are in a "renovation" state of transformation. If our foundation is good, we don't have to demolish everything. But if our foundation is faulty, then we go into a "fix-it" mode, whereas we are ready to repair the foundation prior to re-building the home. Before we start our personal journey of renovation, let's first review what constitutes a good foundation. A firm pedestal consists of; righteousness, integrity, honesty, faith, hope and love. If you are displaying these attributes you have a good foundation.

Now, we will briefly examine each of these character traits. Allow each trait to act as a thermostat to gauge yourself, but NO cheating. Be honest with yourself! The one person you can't run away from is you.

Hope can be defined as; *desire, wish, expectation, yearning and craving.* "Now faith is the substance of things hoped for, the evidence of things not seen," (Hebrews 11:1). Hope is the target of my faith. It tells your faith what to produce. It is the anchor of the soul. An anchor is a devise that prevents you from moving. Hope is my expectation, which paints a picture of how my desire appears. God gave us a guarantee of His Word. Unlike man, God is a promise keeper; His character dictates that He must come through with His Word. Examine what Hebrews 6:17-20 says:

> Wherein God, willing more
> abundantly to shew unto the heirs of
> promise the immutability of his
> counsel, confirmed it by an oath. That
> by two immutable things, in which it
> was impossible for God to lie, we
> might have a strong consolation, who
> have fled for refuge to lay hold upon
> the hope set before us. Which hope we
> have as an anchor of the soul, both

sure and steadfast, and which entered
into that within the veil. Whither the
forerunner is for us entered, even
Jesus, made an high priest for ever
after the order of Melchisedec.

Here, we see there are two components of the
guarantee; He promised and He can't lie. We must believe in
our hearts that all of God's promises are true. We must
meditate with our minds that He can do abundantly above all
we can ask or think. And we must discipline ourselves to
speak only what we want our faith to produce.

Love is defined as; *warmth, affection, attachment, fondness,
tenderness, devotion and adoration.* "Be ye therefore
followers of God, as dear children; and walk in love, as
Christ also hath loved us, and hath given himself for us as an
offering and a sacrifice to God for a sweet smelling savor,"
(Ephesians 5:1). The walk of love is different from the walk
of self. Jesus further explains the importance of love in
Matthew 5:43-48:

Ye have heard that it hath been
said, thou shalt love thy
neighbor, and hate thine
enemy. But I say unto you,
Love your enemies, bless them
that curse you, do good to
them that hate you, and pray
for them which despitefully
use you, and persecute you.

Modern-day Christians think that gossip is
persecution, while the early church died for their faith. This
generation is weaker and wiser, morally dove-like, but
intellectually smart. I believe one of the valuable reasons to

walk in love is preference on this Scripture alone – "But faith worketh by love," (Galatians 5:6). Your faith has its greatest expression through love. When you do something for love, it is accelerated. There is no ulterior motives for what I do, but simply because I love. Love is the Christian icon - AGAPE. Love is not a feeling, it is a choice. The nature of love is giving. It has power over hate, fear, and sin.

Integrity – Are you practicing integrity daily? It is the present commitment to righteousness without compromise. You're right now willingness to do what is right and just in the sight of God. "He who is faithful in a very little thing is faithful also in much; and he who is unrighteous in a very little thing is unrighteous also in much," (Luke 16:10).

Faith – How deep is your faith in God? It is the biblical action of obedience in harmony with the Word of God even in the absence of natural evidence, with the earnest expectation of divine promise being fulfilled. Faith is often a difficult concept to grasp because it requires a strong belief. "Now faith is the substance of things hoped for, the evidence of things not seen," (Hebrews 11:1).

Honesty – How do you define honesty? Is a little white lie still a lie? Small or big – it is a lie. Remember the Ninth Commandment says, "Thou shalt not bear false witness against thy neighbor," (Exodus 20:16).

Commandment says, "Thou shalt not bear false witness against thy neighbor," (Exodus 20:16).

Righteousness – What do you consider righteous behavior? "But seek you first the kingdom of God, and his righteousness; and all these things shall be added unto you," (Matthew 6:33).

Since we have examined our foundation, we are ready to embark on our renovation process. Nothing can ever be achieved without a beginning. You have to start somewhere, so why not here….

The Potter's Wheel

The renovation process starts on the "Potter's Wheel." God knows how to rescue those "voted most unlikely to succeed in life." I believe He enjoys seeing the transformation process of the shunned, looked down upon, and discarded as unprofitable to society. His vision is off the scale, and He knows how to find you in the waste fields of horrific conditions known to mankind.

God gave the Prophet Jeremiah a beautiful illustration of His renovation process for broken and flawed men in the book of Jeremiah 18:1-4:

> Go down to the potter's house,
> and there I will give you my
> message. So I went down to
> the potter's house, and I saw
> him working at the wheel. But
> the pot he was shaping from
> the clay was marred in his
> hands; so the potter formed it
> into another pot, shaping it as
> seemed best to him.

I don't know what needs renovating in your life. However, I know God has a plan to straighten your crooked and marred places! You are on the Potter's Wheel and God is in the middle of reshaping your life. *Be patient. Don't jump off the wheel and prematurely abort the finishing touches that He is completing.*

The Bible talks about, "putting on patience," which denotes that patience isn't something someone else can act out for you. The work of patience can only be completed through your permission and participation. Enough Is Enough! How can you be too weak to make the break, but strong enough to keep bearing the pain? I see this all the time among women who are in toxic relationships. They are using their strength as a means of remaining in bondage, instead of as a way of escape. Every now and then, you win more when you lose. Such is the case with circumstances where we lose those dysfunctional, energy-sucking, relationships. The Bible says, the potter worked the marred clay pot on the pottery wheel and "made it again another vessel." Sounds like renovation to me.

Monuments

The Oxford Dictionary© defines monument as; a marker, shrine, gravestone or tomb. We have erected large, invisible high-risers in our minds that have apparently become insurmountable monuments of destruction. A few years ago, I held a teaching on immovable monuments we placed in our lives. In this particular study, I focused on monuments as being wrong behaviors, ideas, attitudes, motives, and patterns of thinking. Monuments force us to be justified, or operate in defense or denial.

We also place people and relationships as monuments in our lives. Despite how we are treated, we refuse to remove the monuments from their fixed positions in our hearts and minds. Thus, we have become co-dependent on unhealthy relationships. Ultimately, the monuments become humongous, and what began as simple coping mechanisms take on lives of their own. We are on a merry-go-round, and we can't jump off!

It's time to get real. Stop making excuses. Quit trying to defend your unrighteous actions. You need to get real with God. He already knows everything anyway. When we release the right to look good in front of God, we then release our lives from having to defend our actions. Allow your heart to become vulnerable and pliable in the hands of God. You no longer have to camouflage any smell of the flesh.

Repeat the following prayer:

Father, I thank you that my heart is not; unrepentant, unbending, and unyielding. I thank you Lord that my heart is not stubborn, resistant or rebellious to God's ways. I am learning how to be strong, yet flexible; to be bold, yet gentle; to be courageous, yet concerned for others. I strip away every layer and stronghold that has erected itself against the true knowledge of God. Father, pour your grace and mercy into the chambers of my renewed mind, imagination and thoughts. I thank you Father, that your truth is the guiding light of my life and the backbone of my spirit, soul and body. I release myself from artificial life support systems that were used as mediations to replace you and your Word from taking root in my heart. I invite you into the inner and the hidden parts of my life. Let your grace, truth and mercy come into my hidden areas of shame, need and pain. Heal me once and for all. I bind myself to the truth of your Word and I choose to draw all my sustenance from you. All things have become new and I'm living in the newness of life that you have pre-designed for me to live, and it's just a matter of time before I see the full manifestation of your blessings, increase, promotion, and abundance for my life. In Jesus' name.

Now, take a few minutes and praise Him for the manifestation of this prayer . . . Louder! I can't hear you.

No more monuments, procrastination or cop-outs. Get tough with yourself. The human mind, like the human body has an incredible ability to adjust to the demands made on it. When the demands are steady, regular, and consistent, the result is growth, power and greater ease of performance. Make a decision; at least you're moving in some direction. It's time for you to become a participant in God's plan for your life. Remove and block out all distractions and detours. Kick down the red STOP sign! It's time for you to proceed through the green light.

Turn the page – you're headed in the right direction.

Home Renovation

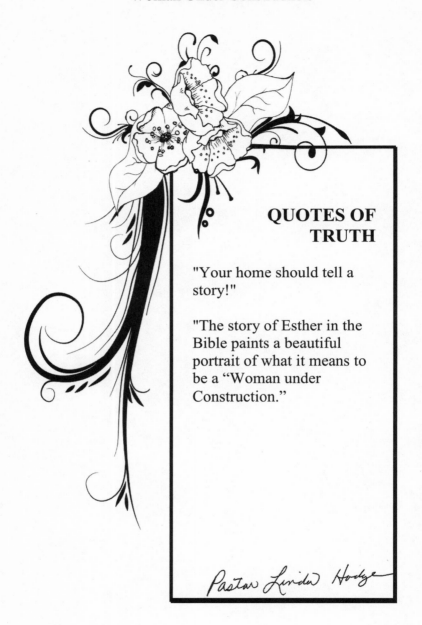

QUOTES OF TRUTH

"Your home should tell a story!"

"The story of Esther in the Bible paints a beautiful portrait of what it means to be a "Woman under Construction.""

Pastor Linda Hodge

Chapter Eight

Create a Stunning Home

Every house possesses exterior esthetics that attract a potential builder. One of the pastime activities that I and my husband enjoy is touring model homes. I suppose we are builders at heart. The difference is we build the lives of people. Nevertheless, while touring these newly-built homes, we not only admire viewing the interior design of homes, but also adore the fabulous exteriors as well. Frequently, we are surprised by the interior style of a house: We had assumed a house would look a certain way based on our observation of the home's exterior.

When house hunting, many are drawn to specific exterior designs of a dwelling. Some favor the majestic Mediterranean- and Tuscan-style homes, while others fancy the traditional Cape Cod or California bungalows. This is all a matter of taste and preference. And of course, there are some who wouldn't care the least, how a house looks on the outside, as long as it suits their tastes on the inside. It's fascinating how a residence can appear smaller than it really is on the inside, or vice versa. Depending upon the home's layout and furnishings, it can appear big or small.

Home builders call the residence's exterior, the elevation. With home buyer incentives, many builders allow buyers to choose their elevation amenities. The usual choices of elevations include; window trim, brick, stucco, as well as the type of garage door, and the front door frame design. Incorporating French doors, plantation shutters, grand porches, terraces, or decks add a sophisticated charm to any home. The exterior finish can be made of aluminum, clapboard, stone, or cedar siding.

There are endless ways to flatter your home. Your schemes may be as simple as resurfacing a driveway or walkway with gravel, slate, brick, or stone. Planting new shrubbery of flowerbeds; applying a fresh coat of paint; putting up new shutters; and creating a new front entrance, all help to update and enhance your home's "curb appeal." However, outer appearances, no matter how graceful, can never replace the absence of the soul and heart that must reside deep inside the interior spaces. The exterior of your house makes a statement to your neighbors. That's all. Your home's outer appearance doesn't physically convey your happiness. It can't reflect your joy as a homeowner. Nor can your home "loudly" echo your sense of personal style.

A shelter, no matter how grand or humble, cannot come to life on its own. Homes are man-made. However, when you observe the appearance, spirit, mood, and vitality of a house, you get an honest feeling for the chemistry of its inhabitants. It is inside the living spaces, where your house can speak your language. Rooms take on your personality, and the colors you choose articulate volumes about your temperament.

Years ago, I invited a lady to lecture at our Women's fellowship on a very interesting topic, "Colors." At the conclusion of the session, each woman was able to identify her color, as it related to her personality. We all left that seminar understanding ourselves a whole lot better. It's interesting when you consider how certain colors convey your type of personality.

I wish I could tell you that once you have "decorated" your house, you are finished and that everything in your life will fall into place. But that's not how life works. We can finish a house, but never a home. There is always continual improvement needed – new styles – remodeling to accomplish. There is always a "new" you evolving. Decorating is a process that should carry on throughout your lifetime. Don't think of decorating, think of creating.

Now, for a few minutes, let's discuss interior design. By the way, did I tell you that interior decorating is one of my favorite pastimes? I love beautifying, both spiritually and naturally as well. We all want our homes to be a true expression of ourselves. Unfortunately, too often, we're timid about designing. "Should we put this here or there? Does this look overly covered in this area?" These are examples of the many questions we sway back and forth, while moving around, pillows, lamps, sofas, throws, etc. And then, there are those either starting out, starting over, or are eager to get going – but become so overwhelmed by the vast range of choices. What colors? What fabrics? What pieces of accessories? Certain folks become paralyzed and give-up.

Taking action is what life is all about. "If you're not moving, you're not advancing." That's one thing that action does; it creates a momentum. In most cases, when momentum starts, it generates a sense of excitement to complete the task.

Discover Your Personal Decorating Style

Style really comes down to what makes you feel good. I've learned that I like earth tones, but I also love to add a little "punch" of color to jazz things up a bit. I throw a little of the unexpected into the mix. Did you know that colors you are fond of wearing may also offer a new impression of comfort in the rooms of your home? As I mentioned earlier, your personality has a way of connecting with your color choices. If you are a naturalist, you probably feel more at home surrounded with subtle tones. You'll probably choose classic, antique furnishings. Or, if you're outgoing and flamboyant, you're most likely drawn to spontaneous, unconventional and abstract pieces.

Whoever you are, do not deny it. Celebrate it! Style emerges when you accept your likes and dislikes. But as you analyze your personal designing style; be encouraged to push that envelope a bit. I noticed that I have done exactly that throughout the years. Recently, I observed that beautiful "lime" color in the stores. So, I began to accessorize that color in a few select places in my living- and family rooms. It brought a sparkle of surprise in the spaces, and was an eye-catcher.

Don't be afraid to contour your environment to suit your unique needs. Go ahead and manipulate your spaces. Break the rules! If one particular room or area of your house can be served better in an unconventional way, utilize the space. It's OK if it's just for a season in your life. My husband and I are presently looking to move from a two-story home, to a single-story dwelling. Over time, both my husband and I have changed our tastes. Now, we really want the "feel" of more open spaces and easy access. If we don't decide to custom build, then we definitely will go in tearing down a few walls to design an environment that is suitable and functional for our lifestyle.

Bring "you" into your home. Your place should tell a story! It should paint a picture of your life's achievements and interests, as well as goals for the future. If you're only surrounded by where you've been, what is your motivation to propel into the future? There should be cruises that you want to take, international tours you're pining to experience, or cars you want to drive in the very near future. Everything is interconnected. Your past and its memorabilia, as well as your faith for tomorrow are all related. *When I visit your house, it should be an experience.*

Now, let's proceed in the latter portion of this chapter exploring and creating a beautiful woman on the outside, as it relates to what's on the inside. In the previous chapters we discussed building from the inside out. At this point, we'll do a paradigm shift. We will take another approach as the outside adornment should reflect a much weightier substance on the inside.

First, we proceed, I need you to know that you are the King's daughter. You must demonstrate His Excellency not only in your spiritual life, but also in your outer adornments. The Oxford Dictionary© defines the word *excellence* as; superiority, high quality, fineness, greatness, prominence, eminence, preeminence, distinction, value, and worth. We will take a closer look at the various beauty facets of a woman, and leave no stone unturned. I hope you are in a comfortable chair, and have your favorite herbal tea! You may want to snuggle up with your favorite blanket. Don't forget your pillow.

Beautifully Arrayed

The story of Esther in the Bible paints a stunning portrait of what it means to be a "Woman under Construction" with respect to her loveliness. Hadassah (or "Esther," as she would become) was a peasant – not at all suitable for the palace. Esther wasn't fit for the King. The same could be said for every female candidate preparing for her "one night with the king." According to Esther 2:2-3 (ESV):

> Then the king's young men who attended him said: Let beautiful young virgins be sought out for the king. And let the king appoint all officers in all the provinces of his kingdoms to gather all the

> beautiful young virgins to the harem in Susa the capital, under custody of Hegai, the king's eunuch, who is in charge of the women. Let their cosmetics be given them. And let the young woman who pleases the king be queen instead of Vashti. This pleased the king and he did so.

Now, don't let this fool you. Ponder over this statement: And let beauty preparations be given them. This was no quick trip to the market. According to biblical accounts, this was a "beauty preparation" that took 12 months! Imagine how it takes nine months to bring forth a child. Then, what type of beauty preparation takes 12 months?

The Bride

The closest resemblance to this is the preparation of the traditional bride-to-be in a wedding ceremony. Whether it is a small or large wedding, the bride has much planning to accomplish before the big day. There are major decisions to be made. Determining the right choice of dress can be a long, tedious ordeal.

"Should I pick the form-fitting, Vera Wang™ silk dress with the fabulous sweetheart tissue organza, neckline? Or, do I want to look like Cinderella, stepping out in my Jessica McClintock™ satin bridal gown with the smart square neck, bubble skirt, and low petticoat. I will need a prince and white, horse-drawn carriage for that dress! Am I making a fashion statement or attempting to be too trendy?

Better yet, should I just think out of the box, and do the unexpected?" At any rate, choosing the right bridal dress can be one of the most tantamount decisions in a woman's life.

I can only imagine that Esther went "bridal shopping" at the Persian equivalent of Saks Fifth Avenue© of New York©, Neiman Marcus©, or perhaps Bloomingdale's©. Maybe, a designer's name similar to the House of Dior©, Versace™, Vera Wang™, Chanel™, or Oscar de la Renta™ was on the list to explore its possible striking gowns. A budget was never mentioned on this shopping spree because each candidate was given the king's American Express™ Black Card, which held an unlimited budget.

There were many decisions to be made, along with choosing an exquisite gown. You must take into consideration the jewels that will accessorize the dress. "Do I want my gems to be simple, yet elegant? Should I go over the top and be flagrant and fabulous?" If you have been a bride, then you know what I'm talking about here. Decisions and preparations are part of the wedding day's total success. You just don't wake up on your wedding day, and decide that very morning what you're going to wear. Nor does the bride say, "I'll take a quick shower and grab something to wear for my honeymoon night." It's best to plan how to style your hair, and what colors you will be wearing to enhance your eyes.

The Bible says that Esther spent 12 months preparing for one night with the king in some unique ways (see Esther 2:12, ESV):

> Each young woman's turn came to go in to King Ahasuerus (Xerxes) after she had completed twelve month's preparation, according to the regulations for the women, for

> thus were the days of their preparation apportioned: six months with oil of myrrh, and six months with perfumes and preparations for beautifying women.

This was no quick random perfume chosen for the day. "Should I wear this one or that one? How do I feel like smelling today?" No, this preparation was no spray on: Or, dabbing on a little here and a little there. It requires a layering regiment of saturation of the various species. These fragrances were to be absorbed in the skin, not just placed on the skin. If it was not properly layered over a cosmetic burner onto the body, covered and shielded it couldn't penetrate the skin pores.

Remember, fragrance was discussed throughout the life of Jesus, from His birth to His burial. The parallels of Esther's preparation; to our Lord's progression; to the "cross of destiny" are remarkable. The spiritual application in reference to fragrance is the anointing. Fragrance in this context is costly, and can't be purchased off a sales rack or replaced with a discount coupon cut from the newspaper or department store sales paper. Myrrh was used as an agent of purification in the process of preparing Esther for one night with the king.

The role of myrrh in the Old Testament sacrifices and in Jesus' life, death, and burial vividly illustrates the concept of killing the old man, removing the blemishes, purging the inner iniquities, and turning away from old practices, habits, mindsets, and limitations. Paul tells us what we should do through his word to the Corinthian church, "We use our powerful God-tools for the truth of God, fitting every loose thought and emotion and impulse into the structure of life shaped by Christ. Our tools are ready at-hand for clearing the ground of every obstruction, and building lives of obedience into maturity" (2 Corinthians 10:4-5, The Message). This says that He has given us weapons and tools for us to use to pull down strongholds, barriers, and obstruction between us and Him. It's like what your Mom would tell you, "You have to lay down in the bed you make." "Whatever you built, you tear down."

Esther's first six months of preparation speaks of cleansing, purification, and the removal of all toxins and defiling agents, both within and on the exterior. Every bridal candidate submitted to extensive preparation to remove order, habit, blemish, or spot that would be out of place before the throne of the great ruler. I know we can go to the MAC™ counter or Bobbi Brown™, or maybe Make Forever, and purchase a concealer in order to cover up our blemishes, but not so for the next Queen of Persia. Esther was washed, scrubbed, and immersed in special cleansing herbs and spices. This was some ancient exfoliation process! Can you imagine how sweet she smelled?

When we soak in His oils of full surrender, accompanied with thanksgiving, praise, and worship, then we exchange our earthly stench for heavenly fragrance. We can actually begin to smell like heaven. I have a few favorite fragrances that I like wearing for various occasions. A few fragrances I wear during the day and others in the evening. Many females are known for the perfumes they wear, have you heard the sayings, "I smelled you, before I saw you?" In other words, your very presence saturates the room. When you are soaked in His presence with a lifestyle of praise and worship, every pore of your skin, secretes the aroma of Him. The very presence of God has a sweet smelling scent. Many depict Him as the Rose of Sharon, and He's the Lily of the Valley.

Spa Day

Several days prior to each encounter with the king, I would assume that the candidates vying for the position of the queen went through a spa day treatment. Their faces were analyzed, to determine what products would be used to accentuate their skin with the perfect glow and texture. The skin preparation would start with a cleansing solution, which is at the core of a traditional beauty regiment. Then the skin is exfoliated with a gritty substance to remove the dead surface layer. At this time, moisturizers were applied to hydrate the skin properly. The ingredients in the moisturizers aid in hydrating the superficial layers.

Their neck and décolletage treatment was a must for their preparation for a night with the king. The neck and chest area are always the-tell-tale signs of aging. Let's not forget about the lips, they can be inviting or repelling. So, the women's lips were conditioned as well and had to be hydrated with a protective balm. The exposure to the harmful ultraviolet rays cause ugly vertical lines to appear around their mouth, thus UV protection was a requirement to invite the king to want to sample their lips.

Another give-away for those aging virgins was their hands. They are prone to liver spots, lines, wrinkles and general dryness. So, it was a standard for all the young women to have treatments of hand cream, or a facial moisturizer with UV protection. Their hands also were treated with a mild body exfoliate once a week. This encouraged the shedding of old skin cells, and the formation of new cells and smooth skin. Such exfoliate is similar to the paraffin-wax hand treatments, which are fabulously moisturizing for the cuticles and surrounding skin, and can be used on hands and feet. By the way, the paraffin-wax hand treatment is one of my favorite spa treatments that I purchase for myself once a month.

Most of us spend hours worrying about our silhouettes, yet we tend to neglect the texture of our skin, which also plays a vital part in the way we look. But, it was not true for these ladies in the Scriptures. During their days at the spa, their time was spent on exfoliating their skin at least once a week. When the king touched their skin, it had to be smooth and soft to his hands.

God's Next Top Model

One of my favorite shows is *America's Next Model©* produced by Tyra Banks. It's a "girly" thing, and I enjoy the whole transformation process. While hundreds of women across the country enter each year, 13 young ladies between the ages of 18 and 27 are selected to compete on the reality show. They live together in a mansion and travel across the world competing for the opportunity to land a major modeling contract.

It's always fascinating to me how the women arrive at an audition for the show appearing one way, and through the process of time, are transformed into this totally different person. Tyra usually jumpstarts their transformation with a haircut, hair color change, or adding a weave (hair extensions) with a top-notch hair stylist. They look over the bone structure of their face, and then begin cutting, weaving and coloring the hair. Some of the girls are literally in tears, especially when inches of hair are being cut away from their security blanket. All they have is the remnants of hair that has fallen on the floor ready to be trashed, never to be seen again.

The model's hair is straightened with a flat-iron or pressing comb. This, in itself, may be an arduous event, depending upon the curliest of the hair, or lets be real and say the "nattiest" of the hair texture, if it needs pressing or just flat-ironed. Some roots of the hair are harder to get straight than other textures. Therefore, more heat is needed to get the desired results.

In life, there are some imbedded deep roots in your subconscious that need to be uprooted. Roots of a tree are symbolic of its foundation. These roots are the building blocks of the tree. Roots pull the nutrients, vitamins, and minerals from the soil to spread life throughout the tree. The only way to kill a tree is to cut its roots. Without roots, a tree cannot live. In fact, when a tree begins to grow – it grows downward (roots) first, and then suddenly it begins to sprout up to penetrate the soil. You grow in a similar manner. So, the question is what are you rooted and grounded in?

When the Holy Spirit begins His transformation process in your life, it can be frightening. *He takes out his surgical instruments and gently begins to cut away layers of your past.* He snips away the roots that have become firmly intertwined with every facet of your life. The Almighty God removes those roots that have sabotaged your growth and caused you not to bear unhealthy fruit in your life!

Let's get back to our model. The appointed staff that is considered the "expert" on training the girls how to walk the platform is added to the sequence of their training regiment. She thinks she knows how to walk; she has been practicing this "walk" for a long, long time. The trainer responds with a sheer grin on his face and says, "You don't know *how to walk* where you are about to *have to walk*. You can't just clomp onto the stage." They literally put a book on the young lady's head and she is taught how to refine her stride so she doesn't bob up and down, or cause the book to fall through sudden or ungraceful movements. She learns exactly how to pivot and turn as if on a fashion runway.

The spiritual correlation to walking is the practical outworking of our heavenly position here on earth. It can also be denoted as our "lifestyle" that we have obtained through Christ. As heavenly women, your earthy conduct

[96]

must exemplify the character of Christ. "This I say... that ye no longer walk as the Gentiles also walk, in the vanity of their mind... But... that ye be renewed in the spirit of your mind," (Ephesians 4:17, 23). The word "walk" literally means "to walk around," and is used here figuratively by Paul to mean; "to deport oneself," and "to order one's behavior."

My spiritual walk with God is not something remote and unreal, to be expressed only in church. It is all about relationships, it's not a façade. *It is very present and practical: It is the real test of our conduct in our relations with others.* Unless we bring heavenliness into our homes, office, shops, kitchens, and practice it there, our walk will be without meaning!

Make-Up Artist

Having the right make-up artist for that special night with the king was invaluable. The perfect make-up artist could enhance your confidence and make an evening with the king exciting before it actually begins. The creaminess of your foundation; the smooth, unbroken texture of your perfectly blended eyelids; and the glossy pout of your mouth (if needed), would garner serious attention to the king's eyes. Perfectly threaded eyebrows zeroed much-needed gazes into soon to be captivating faces.

Ideal shades of eye shadow were selected to enhance Esther's skin tone as well as her gown. A touch of shimmer that gives a playful look was the choice of color for some of the young ladies, while a smokier shadow was applied to others. Maybe, a few wore more of soft, natural tones, which gave a romantic and simple look.

Faces begin as an artist's canvas, but without proper base coat, the skin would not have that sensual glow. So the artist had to experiment with the proper foundation to get the precise, natural look possible. A flawless foundation was chosen. Some of the young ladies wear sheer foundation, oil-based foundation, cream foundation or matt foundation. It was specifically chosen for their skin type.

Esther's finishing touches were completed with powder. This served to set her foundation and to control the shine. The make-up artist completed the canvas with; translucent, pigmented, or powder foundation. A touch of blush was applied and once this was completed, she was minutes away from being in the king's presence.

Before exiting the make-up artist's chamber, Esther's lipstick was applied. I wonder if she wore matte lipstick, opaque, rich, non-shiny shades which lasted the longest. Do you think she was working with a red-lip, or a nude lip with a smoky eye color? Perhaps, she opted for a sheer moisturizing lipstick, which was a bit more casual, and contains moisturizing ingredients like Vitamin E or jojoba oil to keep her lips supple and soft. Lip-gloss could have been chosen as well since it comes in many textures, plus it makes lips look plumper.

My partner in crime, as well as make up junkie partner, Cherie, and I thought that Esther probably kept her make-up to sheer, elegant and romantic shades. Ms. Esther was on a mission that night; to look the best, feel the best, and stand out from the crowd. How you look on the outside, your exterior does make a difference. Pamper yourself, celebrate you, and become the Best You!

Put all of these tips into action. As for your personal residence, allow your spirit to dictate the colors, furnishings, and accessories to ensure that both the interior and exterior of your home represents the real you! Meditate before the artwork and fixtures are placed throughout the living spaces. *Therefore, when visitors enter, it will be an anointed experience.*

Create a Stunning Home

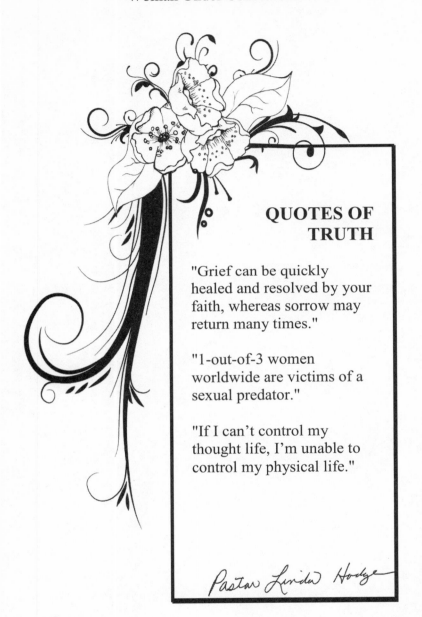

QUOTES OF TRUTH

"Grief can be quickly healed and resolved by your faith, whereas sorrow may return many times."

"1-out-of-3 women worldwide are victims of a sexual predator."

"If I can't control my thought life, I'm unable to control my physical life."

Pastor Linda Hodge

Chapter Nine

Your House Needs First-Rate Piping

V ine's Complete Expository Dictionary of Old and New Testament Words© defines the term "mind" to denote the seat of reflective consciousness, comprising the faculties of perception and understanding, and those of feeling, judging and determining.

The piping of a structure is a channel designed to move resources from one location to another. If it leaks, it can create an overflow of problems. Pipes are hidden in the walls of its buildings. Oftentimes, a great deal of damage has already taken place before a warning signal is known. When you finally realize a piping problem exists, mold has most likely settled in, ruining the wood planks in the edifice. The planks may then need to be aired out, or in some cases, completely replaced. This situation occurred in our charming palatial palace a few years ago. Piping in the master bathroom began deteriorating due to a leak.

A leaky pipe traveled downstairs through the walls, thereby creating further damage to the plumbing in the kitchen. To make matters worse, the pipes that carried hot and cold water in our guest bathroom operated in quite a perplexed manner. The tube that was supposed to carry the cold water was filtering the hot water, and the cold water tube acted as the hot water pipe. I still haven't quite figured out how that problem transpired. Isn't it fascinating for a house to be exceptionally striking on the exterior, but lose its appraisal value when it's discovered that the interior has significant leaky pipes.

Just like pipes run throughout a home, our brain acts as a conductor, sending messages and transmitters via capillaries and blood vessels throughout our bodies. Now, consider the duties of an orchestra conductor. He directs other musicians and writes musical arrangements. His vocation is to keep everyone in sync, harmony and balance. If the conductor doesn't give directions precisely, he could possibly sabotage the performance of the whole orchestra. A flautist, drummer or trumpeter out of sync, or not measuring up to their full potential, could potentially cause the entire orchestra to be in discord and disarray.

Grief, Frustration and Loss

Throughout the piping system of our minds, grief, frustration, and loss must be inspected closely. It's time to unplug the piping system and flush out the clogged debris that is lingering on the subconscious thoughts of our minds. Grief, frustration and loss appear in two forms. There is grief which originates from loss or unachieved aspirations, while frustration occurs from loss of income or a job. These are all hurts in relation to things; a dream or a hope; possibly an object, like a loss of a set of china handed down from a grandparent. As a matter of fact, when my mom passed away years ago, she gave me a few of her "sacred," gigantic cooking pots and pans. I guard them with my life. These items are precious to me simply because they once belonged to her.

So every time I cook a pot of greens or make macaroni and cheese, I recall my mother and her love for cooking. Almost immediately, I am hit with a rollercoaster of emotions associated with grief, frustration and loss. This overwhelming experience simultaneously happens in relationship to God, others or oneself. Of the two, frustration is far more formidable. Lost belongings become only a memory, while God and people continue to live. I have spoken with countless women who have lost a parent, especially in their formative years. They all agree that this kind of bereavement is not like the loss of a limb. One can lose an arm and, nevertheless, adjust because the central core of the person remains intact, along with the supportive systems of friends and relatives.

However, a parent has a far more foundational function in our lives than even our own legs. Since losing my mother, I've realized that while losing a parent because of death is devastating, the lost a parent due to emotional detachment has equally disastrous affects. This is witnessed various times when mothers abandon their daughters for a mixture of unjustifiable reasons. A young child's spirit seeks definition and fulfillment daily from her parents. However, when emotional detachment occurs, immediately a sense of abandonment is introduced to the girl.

There is also a direct correlation of our spirit's health to physical health, especially regarding elderly people. "A good wife is the crown of her husband, but she who brings shame is like rottenness in his bones," (Proverbs 12:4, NLT). Grief from the loss of loved ones affects the physical health of our very bones. Why are bones so important? Check out these simple facts (from the Reader's Digest Medical Encyclopedia):

> Bones are the source of vital
> constituents of blood. They are
> the storehouse from which the
> calcium in blood plasma is
> obtained. The pores and
> cavities are filled with red

marrow. Red marrow consists
largely of blood corpuscles in
all stages of development.
About five million mature red
blood cells are produced and
released every second. The
blood platelets, which are
essential for blood clot
formation; and the white cells
which protect the body against
infection, are also formed in
the red marrow.

I realize some of you have suffered great losses in
your life, but I want to encourage you not to give up, give-in
or give-out! *There is a power available to heal.* Isaiah 53:3-5
(NLT) reminds us:

He was despised and forsaken
of men. A man of sorrows, and
acquainted with grief; And like
one from whom men hide their
face, He was despised, and we
did not esteem Him. Surely our
grief's He Himself bore, and
our sorrows He carried; yet we
ourselves esteemed His
stricken, smitten of God, and
afflicted. But He was pierced
through for our transgressions,
He was crushed for our
iniquities; the chastening for
our well-being fell upon Him,
and by His scourging we are
healed.

Grief can be quickly healed and resolved by your faith, whereas sorrow may return many times. Sorrow and tears are not marks of lack of faith. In fact, sorrow is a healthy release of death and hurt. During the holiday seasons, the loss of a loved one or experiencing an incident that triggers a cherished memory may provoke a person to experience sorrow. The holidays are also the time when survivors of deceased family members need a strong support system to share their emotions. Eventually, this duress will go away – naturally in time – when healing and acceptance are completed in the heart.

My suggestion to you is to release the pockets of sorrow. *Let the tears flow.* I was team-teaching with my husband on a series called, "Bitterness and Regret," when one of the older women in our congregation gave us a praise report. She described how the lesson brought her to a place of release. The member shared with us the staggering pain she had been experiencing due to the loss of her mother more than 10 years ago. During this report, the elder congregant admitted holding herself hostage to the fact that she didn't bring her mom a special dish while the mother was in the hospital prior to dying. The mom told the woman if she didn't bring the meal, then she would not see her alive again! Unfortunately, that was exactly what happened. The woman was struggling to forgive self, and stop the haunting reminder of the incident that occurred year after year. Sadly, dealing with this type of emotional distress occurs in many people when they don't deal with grief and regret. It becomes repressed but is in no way silenced.

My husband and I were recently counseling a young man who was betrayed by his wife. He consciously decided that love costs too much. So, he shut up his heart, making a subconscious decision to never love again or be vulnerable with any woman. His heart became hardened because of the buried sorrow. Fortunately, this young man is now in the healing process because He chooses to allow Jesus, the

Healer, to travel with him to his place of healing and restoration. At times, the pain is so intense, that we deny the Healer, Himself, to mend us. We find it difficult to trust even Him with our pain. Besides, He may require that I leave it at the cross. But my only justification of self-preservation is my ability to take it into my own hands! "This hurts too much to place it within someone else's control!"

Real Issues

Recently, at a "Just Us Girls" ministry service at church, I facilitated a talk-show format. The talk-show panel consisted of women who had experienced heartfelt, life-altering situations in their lives. All of the guest panelists were experts on several topics, including abuse. It was a phenomenal event, and I was thoroughly pleased with the outcome. From drug abuse; to domestic violence; to sexual molestation, we covered the whole gamut. I must admit, I was tremendously surprised from the reaction of the audience, who all had family members combating the deadly pandemic virus of the "drug world."

A number of women admitted to having experienced some form of abuse. Numerous statistics report an alarming number of women are subjecting themselves to abusive relationships. According to the 2005 report, "Worldwide Sexual Assault Statistics," released by the George Mason University Sexual Assault Services, 1-out-of-3 women worldwide are victims of a sexual predator. I, being a victim of both domestic violence and sexual abuse could totally relate.

However, since I was the one facilitating the "talk-show," I desperately attempted to maintain composure, and "look the part," as if I was totally unmoved by the topic. However, underneath the façade, I was replaying my own scarred past. After watching, listening and observing the crowd, I felt compelled to incorporate this special chapter and address "*real issues.*" I have a few crucial points that I believe would be a blessing to you, the reader.

Just think about it, even if you have not been victimized in this way, you definitely know a family member, or a friend who has experienced such harmful circumstances. Moreover, data reveals that a female child is molested every 60 seconds!

Abused women carry tons of unwarranted guilt. First off, there is genuine guilt in terms of anger, hate, and wanting to kill. Perhaps, some even contemplate thoughts of suicide. Second, guilt also proceeds from confusion. A girl who has been sexually abused by a family member or friend feels like she has acted in a certain way to attract that sort of attention. She then feels negative about herself because she was victimized by someone she admired and trusted. Every girl needs to develop a confident and wholesome sense that she is beautiful, loved, and treasured.

Young girls must learn to rest in the loveliness of their Creator. Your dad compliments and reaffirms you as he expresses affection for you. The confidence a girl develops in relation to her father enables her to meet her husband's needs and nurture him in a warm, relaxed freedom, knowing she is a blessing to him. This nurturing happens only if her father responds to her as admirer and *protector*. She will blossom fine as long as her dad; *shields* the beauty he sees developing and unfolding in her; his affection remains clean; and his attention is *trustworthy*.

But if a girl reaches out in a normal, healthy way for appreciation and fatherly affection, and her father (or another male relative) violates the God-given trust he was assigned to protect, then the girl will feel horribly betrayed. If her mother was aware of the abuse, and did not stop it, the girl will experience double betrayal and abandonment. Regrettably, the girl feels guilty for reaching out, needing, and desiring to be considered pretty. She may unconsciously make a promise not to be pretty if beauty attracts nastiness.

Later, when she marries, she may want desperately to embrace her husband fully, but then finds built-in, shut-off mechanisms operating the moment h begins to approach her. She starts to feel unclean from the "stench" left years earlier by the predator. Thank God for the cleansing water of the Living Word! The Word is more powerful than bleach and washes away all stenches! Imagine seeing volumes of Living Water washing over, in and through you until you are "squeaky clean."

"What God has cleansed, no longer consider unholy," (Acts 11:9). If you are a victim, I pray that the walls of isolation, which have been built to hide your shame, are melted down. I pray that you are set free and come forth as pure, refined gold.

One woman that I chatted with had been sexually abused by numerous male relatives. Therefore, she found it difficult to be romantic with her husband. Through prayer, her wounds began to close. Layer by layer, she gained the strength to fortify her spirit. She was then able to risk opening her heart to trust, and to give herself to her husband. *Her spirit had to be loosed from the ones who violated her.* The sword of truth in the hand of the Lord Jesus, cleaving between her and her abusers, ripped away roots that had been buried and hidden. Although she will never forget the incident, God's healing grace allows her to recall memories without feeling unclean.

The Scriptures in Luke 6:45 tell us to thoroughly examine the source of our problems: "The good man out of the good treasure of his heart brings forth what is good; and the evil man out of the evil treasure brings forth what is evil; for his mouth speaks from that which fills his heart." Unbelievably, we begin to store treasures in our heart from the moment we become a living being. Our treasure consists of every experience, response, attitude, judgment and expectation we possess. In the book of Luke, Jesus isn't withholding anything when speaking to the Christians that are already committed to Him and call Him, "Lord." Luke 6:46-49 reads:

> And why do you call me,
> "Lord, Lord," and do not do
> what I say? Everyone who
> comes to Me, and hears My
> words, and acts upon them, I
> will show you whom he is like:
> he is like a man building a
> house, who dug deep and laid a
> foundation upon the rock; and
> when a flood arose, the torrent
> burst against that house and
> could not shake it, because it
> had been well built. But the
> one who has heard, and has not
> acted accordingly, is like a
> man who built a house...
> without any foundation; and
> the torrent burst against it and
> immediately it collapsed, and
> the ruin of that house was
> great.

Yes, there are fractures in your early foundations, caused either by wounds inflicted upon you, or by your sinful responses to events in your life. We are often broken by those events, and it weakens our ability to stand in the time of trial or in the face of a crisis. I want you to know that because you are born anew in Jesus, you are in the position to start over! Your foundation is re-built upon the Rock who is Jesus!

The Law of the Spirit vs. The Law of the Flesh

In the book of Romans, chapter eight speaks explicitly about the mind. Paul begins his salutation addressing the law of the spirit versus the law of the flesh.

> For those who live according
> to the flesh set their minds on
> the things of the flesh, but
> those who live according to the
> Spirit, the things of the Spirit.
> For to be carnally minded is
> death, but to be spiritually
> minded is life and peace,
> (Romans 8:5, 6).

When you choose to walk after the spirit, you're setting your mind on the things of the spirit; which denotes that the spirit is ruling, instead of your fleshly desires, appetite, or passions. The word "*rule*" means; governing power or its possession; use of authority; the duration of such power; an authoritative, prescribed direction for conduct, especially one of the regulations governing procedure in a legislative body; or a regulation observed by the players in a game, sport, or contest.

We can also say whoever is ruling, calls the shots in your life. "*Walking*" by the spirit simply means that my mind has been submitted under the lordship of Jesus Christ. Essentially, your mind is spirit-controlled. I choose by an act of will to "set" my mind to live according to the spirit. The Heritage Dictionary© defines the word "set" as; to put in a specified position; place; to put into a specified state; to put into a stable position; to fix firmly or in an immobile manner; to restore to a proper and normal state when dislocated or broken; and to adjust for proper functioning.

[110]

Whatever the mind sets itself on becomes a person's *walk*. If the mind is consumed with the flesh, we walk after that; conversely, if it sets itself upon the spirit, we follow after it.

Our minds are continually "under construction," and constantly retrieving, sorting, filtering and analyzing new information. Simultaneously, our minds are disarming, dismantling, and capturing other unfruitful information that attempt to seep its way into our subconscious. Watch out! Harmful information can get a footing and create mass destruction for your life. An idea can be initiated from; God, Satan, ourselves, or others. It can either grow or start expanding its wings to encompass a large amount of space in our minds. If unsafe data is permitted to "camp out," and if not eradicated upon invasion, it will begin immediately to germinate. Or, it can be arrested upon entrance and discarded from our memory bank.

If I can't control my thought life, I'm unable to control my physical life. Thus, I'm living on impulse and response, and not according to Godly principles. Peter says, "Gird up the loins of your minds," (1 Peter 1:13). The Heritage Dictionary© defines "gird" as; to encircle with a belt or band; to fasten or secure (clothing, for example) with a belt or band; to surround, to equip or endow; to prepare (oneself) for action; to prepare for action; and to summon up one's inner resources in preparation for action.

We must keep our minds in the peace of God at all times. "You will keep him in perfect peace, whose mind is stayed on you, because he trusts in you," (Isaiah 26:3). A disturbed brain can be dangerous in many ways. I have spoken to numerous people who had reached the brink of suicide. The common thread that I hear from each one is, "My mind was consumed with these thoughts of constant defeat, no way out, no resolve, no hope, and no escape from tormenting thoughts."

Paul made it very clear on what and how to think. Philippians 4:6-8 (NLT) states:

Be anxious for nothing, but in
everything by prayer and
supplication, with
thanksgiving, let your requests
be made known to God; and
the peace of God, which
surpasses all things, will guard
your hearts and minds through
Christ Jesus. Finally, brethren,
whatever things are true,
whatever things are noble,
whatever things are just,
whatever things are pure,
whatever things are of good
report, if there is any virtue
and if there is anything
praiseworthy – meditate on
these things.

God never intended for you to be fearful, worried
or anxious. It is not His will for you to walk the floors at
night worrying about your children, finances, or spouse.
He has not planned for your mind to be in constant
turmoil. God wants you to lean on His everlasting
tranquility if you lose your job, battle sickness or face
disease.

He has planned for your heart and mind to be
clothed with HIS PEACE! Without God's peace covering
your heart and mind, you will be weakened and
unprepared to face Satan's attacks. If your mind is in
turmoil, right now, I want you to make a determination to
take the peace God has promised you and clothe your
mind with it!

Today is the day to no longer experience warfare.
Today is the day to stop accepting your present,

temporary situation as your future, permanent situation. *Despite your current circumstances, make up your mind to get on with your life.* Fulfill your divine purpose and calling.

Today is the day to walk by faith – right out of your present circumstances!

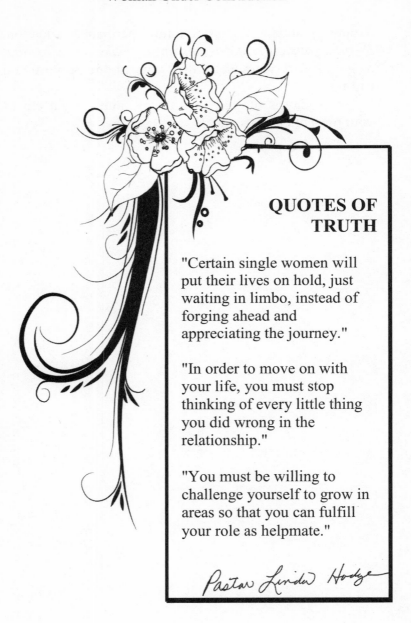

QUOTES OF TRUTH

"Certain single women will put their lives on hold, just waiting in limbo, instead of forging ahead and appreciating the journey."

"In order to move on with your life, you must stop thinking of every little thing you did wrong in the relationship."

"You must be willing to challenge yourself to grow in areas so that you can fulfill your role as helpmate."

Pastor Linda Hodge

Chapter Ten

The Heart of the Home

Single and Satisfied

The Bible examines the concept of how a woman builds her home through an interesting passage of Scripture found in Proverbs 14:1 which reads, "The wise woman builds her house, but with her own hands the foolish one tears her's down." For this particular chapter, we will use the analogy of the kitchen, as a means of relating to the various facets of a woman. We will look at women who are single, divorced, aspiring to become married, or are presently married. Her actual state is the core of her values with respect to her aspirations and ambitions.

Similarly, the construction of a dwelling's kitchen is extremely pivotal, where the kitchen is the heart of a home. The kitchen is an awesome place for ministry, as you can devote a great deal of preparation and love into each planned meal. Its inviting space allows you to fellowship with family members and strangers about the love of Christ. While at the same time, arousing their taste buds with exotic and delicious flavors. Stirring herbs into hearty dishes that release pleasant aromas, will kick the sensory system into high gear, and beckon everyone to the dining table. Memorable family meals have a lasting effect on all.

Thus, most homebuyers' main concern is the kitchen. Beyond the desired Sub-Zero™, stainless steel appliances, buyers check for the overall layout and what it may take to bring the kitchen up to par. Is the kitchen U-shaped and opens into the family room? Or, is it galley-style with free-flowing outlets? Numerous homeowners enjoy interacting with guests and cooking simultaneously. Thus, they seek gourmet kitchens that have breakfast bars and kitchen islands. Some are attracted to a pantry, plenty of cabinet space, featuring high quality   finishes, such as; cherry, maple, antique white or frosted glass.

You might prefer black-and-white speckled granite to yellow tile for your kitchen countertops. Others admire floors covered with the Southwestern style of ceramic Terra Cotta tile, elegant marble or warm hardwood. When you begin to address your kitchen's layout, you must decide on the look you want to represent your heart. Is it country and casual, sophisticated and sleek, minimalist and industrial, or contemporary and open?

In comparison, when you design your life as a single, divorced, want to be married or a married woman, ample consideration should be taken into account. How are you building the core of your present state? What materials are you using during this construction to become the best YOU possible? Within the following pages, we will explore the required materials for building wholesome, single, divorced, and aspiring to be married, as well as married women.

In this portion of the chapter, I'm specifically writing for the single woman. It's just you and me having a girly chat. Of course, every woman can benefit from this conversation – even if you're not single. You can share these tidbits with your cousins, sisters, nieces, and aunts.

First, before we proceed into the chapter, I want to give you a "thumbs-up" for holding your own. Consider Philippians 4:11 that says, "Not that I speak in respect of want; for I have learned, in whatsoever state I am, therewith to be content." That right there, is a mouth-full. Let's set the record straight. *Being content in your state of singleness does not mean you desire to be single the rest of your life.* It simply means that I choose to remain; cool, calm and collected. YES, you can do this! And all the single women say, "AMEN!" Perfect. I hear you loud and clear!

So now you're thinking, "While I'm cool, calm and collected, exactly what am I supposed to be doing?" That's an excellent question. So let's address it. I need you to throw away your "hit list." The first goal on your list is probably, "tall, dark and handsome." Many of you adore the following; medium build, caramel complexion, bald, a little stocky, and at least six-feet tall. "When I wear my 4-inch platforms, I still want him an inch or two taller than me." I totally understand.

If you can, for a moment, think about readjusting your criteria. Try to encompass some "real substance" for the brother to possess. Throw away the pipe dream of Mr. Right in shining armor, riding on his white horse, to rescue you from life. He may be your favorite basketball or football player, or your favorite music artist. And when he sings, his smooth tenor vibrato sends thrills down your spinal cord. Hello? Let's get real here. We need to consider what assets you bring to the relationship. By assets, I am not necessarily speaking of material assets, (although they can be considered). Listen. What emotional, spiritual, intellectual and yes, physical attributes do YOU posses that will be comparable to your potential mate?

You also need take into consideration whether he can spiritually cover you. He could potentially be a smothering lid, designed to keep you from fulfilling your true potential and drain you of your spiritual prowess. Will your new mate be intimidated by your strength because he is a weak and insecure man? And, will you have to go into a pain staking dialogue with him every Saturday night, "Now honey, don't forget we have church in the morning. So don't stay up too late. Besides, I have already laid out your suit. All you have to do is get up, take your shower and get dressed." Sooner or later, this Saturday night discourse will turn frustrating for both you and your mate.

I hear these scenarios countless times during counseling sessions, where couples are trying to patch up failed relationships. Please don't be one of those statistics. If you are discontent being single, now is not the time to entertain the thought of getting married. I always say, "If you're hungry, any and everything looks good!" You can't be desperate and searching for a man at the same time. In time of desperation you will allow anyone to fill the void. Before you are ready to embrace someone else, you first have to embrace yourself. Being happy and enjoying your single status is too critical. Far too many single women think they can't be happy until Mr. Right comes along. Certain single women will put their lives on hold, just waiting in limbo, instead of forging ahead and appreciating the journey.

Whatever crack is open in the door of your emotions, the enemy is sure to find it. You must deal with any discontent. The Word says, "We are complete in Him, perfect and entire, wanting nothing," (see James 1:4, NLT).

Say this aloud: Father, I thank you that I am content in you. Dear Lord, you are all I need until you see that I am ready for my man of God.

Satan uses the lie of loneliness to put men and women of God into a panic. So what do you do? In order to fill that empty void, many of us spend consistent, intimate time with hamburgers and fries every night before going to bed. Others fall into fornication to prove that they are desirable, attractive and still "got it going on." But, after the sex act is over, Satan is laughing and rolling on the floor. On the contrary, there are countless more of you who refuse to fall prey to the lies and deception of the enemy. You know who you are in Christ and refuse to be caught in the bait of the enemy. Please know that the enemy can't trick you without your permission and participation. Don't give him any power or place.

If your weakness is that tall, dark, handsome, muscle-bound, eye-catching stallion, then believe he will find his way to your doorstep. Pay close attention to what you allow to enter your eye gate; what you read; watch on television and see at the movies. When those attacks (lies) of loneliness and sexual urges come upon you, and then run quickly to the Word of God. If you are saved and filled with the Holy Spirit, you have all the power you'll ever need to defeat the enemy. Take control over your thoughts with 2 Corinthians 10:5, which states, "Casting down imagination and every high thing that exalted itself against the knowledge of God, and bringing into captivity every thought to be obedience of Christ."

Satan's sole purpose is to keep you bound and defeated. However, the power of God is ever-present and able to break and destroy any yoke that may attempt to bind you. That same anointing will set you free to the point you will never be afflicted by that yoke again.

When my husband and I met, I was a hot mess! I was broken in pieces from making serious relationship choices! Obviously, I wasn't saved at the time, so I hadn't a clue what to look for in a mate. My previous relationships were very abusive, to say the least. I was the typical young girl raised by a single mom, who for all intents and purposes, raised her children to the best of her ability. As a result, I transitioned into adulthood ill equipped, and misinformed on how to make wise decisions. Unfortunately, when my husband and I met, I didn't know how to act.

I was so accustomed to worldly men being unfaithful, unholy, and unreliable that I didn't know whether to run or stay. Here was this magnificent God-fearing man, who was a gentleman, and peaceful ruler. He was a wonderful father to his four children, whom his previous wife had abandoned. My husband was nothing that I had experienced in the world.

As I reflect back 29 years ago, I can honestly say my heart was so open to God. My ultimate desire was to please Him, and He began to show me precisely His will for my life. When your heart is right before God, and your chief joy is to please Him, I guarantee, He will show you His Mr. Right for your life!

Now, this next bit of information is imperative for your spiritual walk. It's seriously important that you dress yourself properly each morning. Don't leave the house without putting on your spiritual armor according to Ephesians 6:11-17:

Helmet of Salvation: You are delivered from the power of darkness and everything that originates from the dark realm. You are delivered from the spirit of fear (2 Timothy 1:7 and Romans 8:15). Your helmet provides you divine protection from those attacks that would love to keep you in bondage of hopelessness, fear of not getting married, not being good enough, not looking good enough, unworthiness, and self-sabotage.

Breastplate of Righteousness: You are delivered from condemnation (Romans 8:1), guilt, inferiority complexes and everything that would make you feel less than the righteousness of God in Christ Jesus. You are forgiven from past sins, mistakes, unhealthy alliances, and soul-ties.

Loins gird with the Spirit of Truth: You are delivered from the dominion of the old man with his carnal nature. You do not have to be dominated by your sexual nature of anything else that is not in line with God's character. The truth of God's Word brings wholeness, stability and it encourages you to think like God thinks; love what He loves; and hate what He hates.

[120]

Feet shod with the preparation of the Gospel of Peace: You are delivered from confusion, strife (James 3:16) and anything that is contrary to peace (Romans 12:18). Therefore, as you acknowledge Him in all your ways, He will direct your steps. Your foot will not be caught and entailed in any prohibited and forbidden relationships, and you are delivered from all toxic relationships.

Take up the shield of faith: The just shall live by faith. You will wear your armor by faith. Through the eyes of faith, you will call those things that are not as though they were. Mountains must be removed, strongholds must be destroyed, and every weapon that is formed against you, shall be destroyed. We render it powerless and non-effective.

The Sword of the Spirit: You will use your Sword, the Word of God, as a weapon against the enemy. You shall cut to pieces every unfruitful and beneficial word that has been spoken against you and your success. Your sword of the Spirit is the final authority to settle any questions, situations, conditions, and circumstances that you will ever encounter.

Remember, the violent taketh by force. Whatever the enemy has stolen from you; your self-esteem, joy, or peace – take it back by force in the name of Jesus! You may be waiting on your Mr. Right, but while you're waiting, you are single and whole. Nothing is missing and nothing is broken.

I DON'T WANT TO BE DIVORCED!

Nearly every woman's response to the idea of being divorced has probably been, "I don't want to be divorced." The majority of divorcees did enjoy moments of being married despite the reason for the break-up; adultery, gambling, drugs, pornography, or living with a workaholic.

In the end, all agree that the most painful part of splitting up is dealing with rejection. Your marriage could've been deteriorating for a long time, yet realizing that you're unwanted by your spouse is an extremely hard pill to swallow. Many women, though signs are evident, tend to hold on to broken relationships.

However, I do feel that any marriage can be repaired, as long as both parties are willing to put in the effort. The one that betrays the trust is the one that should devote more time in mending the shattered pieces. After all, the person you vowed to spend the rest of your life with is now being detached from your life. So here you are in shock, denial, and numb. Where do you go from here? What's going to happen to the children? These are only a few questions that arise during this intense, transitional process.

Several women find themselves unable to concentrate: They are too busy thinking of ways to make their spouses suffer. Many do random drive-bys of their spouse's house or office. Several women begin to neglect themselves, their children and everyday obligations. You might become overwhelmed, are unable to sleep, and feel as if the world is closing in on you. Numerous women start avoiding places where she and her husband would frequently visit. And then, there are others who forget important tasks, dates, and commitments. They are unable to tolerate both noise and silence, and lose their temper constantly.

Nevertheless, don't feel like you're losing your mind. It is normal to zoom through the emotional scale or somewhat veer off the scale of emotional instability. Isaiah 43:2 (ESV) is a powerful scripture to meditate upon during these tough times. It reads:

> When you pass through the
> waters, I will be with you; and
> when you pass through the
> rivers, they will not sweep

over you. When you walk
through the fire, you will not
be burned; the flames will not
set you ablaze.

Your mind is rejecting the idea, and your heart can't accept the fact that you will no longer be Mrs.... It's like a heart-transplant, where the body doesn't want to accept the new heart. The body receives it as a foreign object, and it works everyday trying to eliminate it from the body. Therefore, medication has to be given to the patient, in hopes that the body will resolve favorably to the newly acquired heart.

Similarly, in the case of divorce, a wife is traumatized when she is notified that her marriage is soon to be dissolved. She rejects the idea, promising to herself that he will be back. The wife then attempts to convince herself, "This is something he is going through temporarily. We have been together for over 15 years! He can't replace me. I'm the mother of his children." She is in deep denial, and begins to develop a coping mechanism to deal with this newfound loss. For example, she may begin calling her in-laws more frequently, hoping to stay connected with the family.

Listen. In order to move on with your life, you must stop thinking of every little thing you did wrong in the relationship. Sure, you made some mistakes, but remember it takes two mature adults to make a relationship work. It is not solely the responsibility of one individual. Women, in general, accept a great deal of the marriage's failure. "If only if I would have dressed more attractively. I should have lost weight. I shouldn't have complained so much." The list goes on and on....

Let's chat a minute about the kids. Children are the most important variable in this entire equation! I see so many couples fighting, with little concern about the well-being of their heartbroken children. Many think it's OK to belittle, criticize, or berate their former spouses in front of the children. Then, have the nerve to get the children to "take sides!" Unfortunately, the offspring become the battleground.

Please don't use drop-off and pick-up times as an opportunity to argue and fight. This is not helpful for the children and way to dramatic! The best thing two divorced parents can do is allow their kids to see them as loving parents. It's difficult enough to not have both parents in the same home, operating as a healthy and upright family unit. Remember, you are creating daily memories with your children, while their lives are dismantling at the same time. Your child's whole foundation is being uprooted. When this happens, kids start questioning their own identity. At this critical time in a child's life, there must be ongoing communication and affirmation, encouraging them that everything is going to be alright. In some cases, a Christian child-therapist could prove to be very helpful. You must reassure your son that he is accepted and loved by both you and your husband.

Give your children a simple explanation for the divorce. Let them know they are free to love both parents. Kids need to be affirmed and reaffirmed that just because the marriage is over, it has no bearings on their relationship with the other parent.

In order to move on from your marital state to a healthy, single state, self-examination is required. We must sort out this unfortunate, horrible time in your life. You need to look back on the marriage to determine what actually went wrong. A lesson unlearned is bound to be repeated. You can become a better person if you use what you learned to make changes. As you reflect on your past, I'm sure you'll discover that poor communication has been one of the cohorts in the marriage break-up.

Another major element in a marital break-up is getting hitched for the wrong reasons. Innumerable amounts of people enter into marriage with unreasonable

[124]

expectations. Scores of women base their total happiness on the expense of the man. That is why I tell women all the time, "If you aren't happy with yourself, no one else can make you happy." Since no one is perfect, you are certain to be hurt, disappointed, and misunderstood. Heartbreak is and will always be part of life – period. Broken trust is often a primary reason for the failure of a marriage. Once trust is broken, it's like glass – almost impossible to put back together. This is especially true if the severity of the broken glass is busted in minuscule pieces.

For those recently divorced or on the brink of divorce, you may wonder, "Where do I go from here?" Well, you first must accept the fact that you are single or soon to become single. This is not the end of your life! Your destiny consists of more than being married. *It's time to make the most of this fresh start in your life.* Accept the present and use this opportunity for personal and spiritual growth. Develop your spiritual gifts and get involved in ministry or some organization where you are giving. Establish plenty of healthy relationships. *Constantly repeat affirmations of peace over your life.*

"And the peace of God, which transcends all understanding, will guard your hearts and your minds in Christ Jesus," (Philippians 4:7).

Believe me, this thorny part of your life will have closure. It won't be the same, but it doesn't mean that it can't be better. When I divorced, I never thought in a million years that my life would turn out like this. I never dreamed of having such an incredible, God-fearing man in my life. God has done more than I ever could have imagined. My prayer for you is that God, does exceedingly, abundantly more than you could ever imagine. The past is behind, so look beyond the pain, disappointments, and the shattered fairytale dream. There is a new day dawning, right beyond the horizon!

So You Want to be MARRIED?

Today's society, through the various Internet dating websites, is promising both men and women they are guaranteed to find true love. Sure, I have heard both positive and negative responses from individuals who have dared to take the risk. Some have found the love of their life, while others were tricked, schemed and defrauded in believing they were getting Mr. Right. Unfortunately, he didn't fit the total bill. We have become naïve to the fact that just because it looks good on paper, doesn't mean that in actuality it is a match made under heaven.

By answering a questionnaire, dating websites promise to locate the perfect man or woman of your dreams. These questionnaires are designed to identify similarities between you and a prospective partner. You soon realize that compatibility involves far more than having things in common. Ideally, the number one question should be about REAL spiritual commitment. Without the fundamental element of your belief being in common, you are in for a rollercoaster ride through life. Chemistry, complementarily, and comparability are vitally important to any lasting relationship.

Chemistry is not always a good judge of character. It is sometimes referred to what we call, *"love at first sight."* It sees what it wants to see. But once the other side is revealed, those wonderful characteristics vanish like the clouds. Why are we attracted to one person over another? The only answer I can come up with is we have our own issues. Somehow, we formulate in our mind, what, and who can fill that empty love tank we are carrying around. So, you have to address and fix your own issues before you explore the possibility of marriage. I speak to various women who prefer to look for a *bargain* of a man. You should never settle or compromise your standards. And the strange thing about it is your potential "love at first sight" comes in all sizes, shapes, educational backgrounds, and financial situations. No one is exempt from falling in the trap of *"temporary insanity."*

Complementarily refers to the extent to which differences benefit both partners. Two people are usually drawn together by their similarities and their differences. Who wants a "yes man" as a partner to process duplicate thoughts in their minds? Life will start to look boring and all the same shades of color. Plus, why would you want to marry your own reflection? I know you may have felt that you found Mr. Right in a matter of a few minutes of you initially meeting him. Before you say, "I do," please reflect a while on his personality, values, and family background before you make the commitment to marry. Of course, we all have weaknesses but think about this? "Can I live with him and what are my deal breakers in a relationship?" If there aren't any boundaries set, then you are sure to be violated in some form or another. *Here's the real test: Are you a better person with your spouse?*

Comparability is the differences between the two that makes for a good relationship. Check out his personality, and his *emotional temperament*. Is he extroverted or introverted? Warm or cold? Loud or quiet? Expressive or suppressive? Please don't overlook the quality of being mentally and emotionally healthy. Emotionally healthy individuals make better marriage partners than those who have emotional problems. You don't have to be a rocket scientist to know you married a crazy person. Most likely, you will have an insane marriage! Watch out for emotional patterns. It may take several months for a destructive emotion to surface. I have heard numerous news interviews report of women who had been married for extended periods of time, and then they are unexpectedly hit, slapped or thrown across the room.

In certain cases, such abused women are close to the edge of death. Also, please pay special attention to his thinking style, ability to solve problems, and reasoning skills. Is he a visionary? The last thing you want is an immature mind trying to lead you. If he doesn't have the ability to intellectually stimulate and challenge you as a person to do and be better, problems will arise. A great part of marriage is mental, so make sure that you and your spouse have a good meeting of the minds. A spice of humor goes a long way. That is one of the many qualities that I love about my husband. His humor takes me off the serious elements of life at the perfect times.

Explore the values that he and you share. What are your beliefs about marriage? Does he believe that marriage is like a hobby? Is marriage put up on a shelf and removed at your discretion? I am alarmed at the number of men who believe they've been called to the "cummerbund" or polygamy ministry. Sadly, The HBO TV series, *Big Love* has not helped men in remaining faithful to their wives. The show depicts the Mormon Christianity belief that men can have several wives, including children from these various wives. They are considered one happy family. Few boundaries are established – only the fact, that they live in separate houses.

Another strong value that must be explored is how does he manage his finances? Does he believe in tithing and giving? How is his credit rating? Does he need another paycheck the day after payday? All these things must be considered before entering into an emotional attachment. Once the attachment is firm and solid, it is extremely difficult to pull away from the relationship.

Actions Speak Louder than Words

Don't be duped into believing him when his actions are completely contrary to what he is saying. Have you heard the saying, "Your actions speak so loudly, I can't hear what you're saying?" When you remain in a relationship like this, self-doubt begins to surface. He may even try to convince you that you shouldn't believe what you just saw. *Don't listen with your emotions, listen with your eyes.* If he doesn't treat friends in ways that you admire, then what makes you think he will do this with you? Another strong character indicator of whether he is a potential mate is by looking at his friends. Consider the old axiom, "Birds of a feather flock together."

Basically, we associate with people who are similar to us in values, attitudes, personality, age, status and lifestyle! Certain people just aren't good marriage material! They are selfish by nature, and always looking to receive something that they themselves aren't willing to give up. Listen! Don't turn you head toward the *red light*.

Once you have "fallen in love," it is difficult to be sufficiently objective, reasonable, and logical. Emotions flutter and reasoning goes out the window; the heart dominates the head. When you are in love, you'll have a tendency to overlook faults, ignore danger signals that are obvious to others, and to dismiss the counsel of mature persons. So take heed to the deceptively little things that may pop up from time to time. Use wisdom when choosing a mate. *Keep your criteria before you at all times and stick with it.*

This concludes the portion of this chapter on, "So You Want to be MARRIED." I hope you received a few nuggets to help you sort out a few concerns you may have been experiencing. Maybe, this is confirmation that you are on the right track. Now, let's proceed to the section for intended for married women. For all the married women and wanna-be's this is a MUST read portion.

Happily Married After

The final section of this chapter is directed expressly to the "married ladies." If you are a newlywed, or have been married for an extensive period of time, this information will be invaluable to your continual marital success. Great marriages aren't developed overnight, nor do bad marriages crumble suddenly. Marriage is a continual progression of either going upward or downward. You just don't wake-up in the morning and immediately have a good or bad relationship. Circumstances have been manifesting through the process of time to get you where you are today.

Before we proceed further, let's remember what the Scriptures say about marriage: "And the LORD God said it is not good that the man should be alone; I will make him a help meet for him," (Genesis 2:18). The Bible also says, "The man who finds a wife finds a treasure, and receives favor from the LORD," (Proverbs 18:22, NLT). Your value to your husband is indescribable, uncanny, and is the most important relationship he will ever experience in his life. You are bone of his bone; a necessary part of him that he cannot effectively live without. You are a complement, an indispensable resource. You are the BOMB!

So, with all this power I possess, "How am I supposed to use it to build him up?" The last reminding pages will address that question precisely.

You must be his Encourager. The male ego can either be demolished by his wife or built up by her. The word "encouragement" means; to give courage, hope or confidence to, give support, be favorable, and foster help.

My husband always asks me after he has ministered, "How did I do?" No matter what others say to him, what I tell my husband has the most lasting affect. Therefore, I choose to be his best cheerleader, rooting him on, staying attentive while he's ministering and displaying a look of, "I got your back baby! You go boy!" With that type of encouragement sitting on the front row, he can't help but to do his best. Ultimately, he's a blessing to our congregation. *God has given us the power of influence.* When God wanted to change the course of history, He often placed a man or woman in a position of influence, such as He did with Joseph, Daniel, Esther and Nehemiah. God has given you the role to influence your husband in a positive and effective way. You can actually empower him to become the best man possible. Recognize what God wants to do in his life, and water that potential with words of encouragement and affirmation!

The Bible says, "She opens her mouth with wisdom, and on her tongue is the law of kindness," (Proverbs 31:26).

Be sexually open and free. Encouragement and being sexually open and free go hand-in-hand. It's not the plan of God for you not to have good sex. Therefore, make it a priority. Discuss it and make it plain and clear, so there is no room for open doors. It actually satisfies his sexual drive. Sex fulfills his male ego by allowing him to demonstrate his role as husband and lover. It definitely reduces friction in the home and provides one of life's most exciting experiences. *It's OK to be "sexy" for your husband.* Dress the part for him; speak "sweet nothings" in his ear. Don't let him leave the house "hungry," (you know what I mean). Sally Mae is lurking around the corner when he drives out the garage, to "feed him" a homemade meal, and (you know what I mean). So fill him up to the overflow. You are his answer for every desire he may have.

Intelligent and Sharp. You must be willing to challenge yourself to grow in areas so that you can fulfill your role as a helpmate. Don't limit yourself to a small existence of knowing how to make spaghetti. That was good for you to prepare during your first year of marriage. Now is the time to upgrade your repertoire of recipes. Purchase some cookbooks, watch the *Food Network* and begin experimenting. He will enjoy sampling your new dishes. Life doesn't stop once you get the title of wife. You have untapped potential that's ready to come forth. Take an interest in your husband's hobbies and ventures, even if you have loads of clothes to wash, or food to prepare. Take time out to become knowledgeable about his job. In this way, you will have more to communicate with him effectively. At the same time, he will be overjoyed that you took the opportunity to be interested in what his job entails. And finally, be resourceful. Go out and research. Make things happen. This will sharpen him and push him to reach further and expand his horizon as well. Together, you are creating your own legacy!

Disciplined. Take care of your body, through exercise, and eating nutritious meals. I know age accumulates inches, but they don't have to find a resting home in your thighs and hips. Join a gym; take a walk through the neighborhood. Besides, he needs you to be healthy and live a long productive life. Stay disciplined in your spiritual life. The last thing he needs is an emotional, unstable, and unpredictable woman he always has to rescue from anxiety and depression. You are the caretaker of the home. Therefore, if you are out of commission, who will take care of the family? 2 Timothy 1:7 (AMP) reminds us:

> For God did not give us a spirit
> of timidity (of cowardice,
> craven and fawning fear) But

> (He has given us a spirit) of
> power and of love and of calm
> and well balanced mine and
> discipline and self-control.

The antidote to fear is trusting God. He is the ultimate source of all life's problems.

Secure. Most men, like all of us, want to know what to expect. Maintain consistency and predictability. He shouldn't have to question whom he is returning home to each day. Whether you are the loving wife, that he adores, or the frantic disorganized wife that doesn't recall the last place she went. He shouldn't be greeted by the picky, clean freak that screams at the children for leaving their dirty socks on the floor. Your husband wants to know that you are mature and stable. He needs to be assured that you can handle any situation in an intelligent, levelheaded manner.

Fun and Happy. Choose to be a happy person; lighten up with life. Everything is not always as it appears. Your husband wants a fun-loving wife to greet him when comes home from work. He is in a war zone in the world; make his home a place of refuge. I know life can throw some curve balls, but whatever ball you get, you can knock it out the ballpark! Many illnesses are due to unhappiness and holding grudges. Let go of bitterness. The Bible says in Ephesians 6:12, "For we wrestle not against flesh and blood, but against principalities, against powers, against the rulers of the darkness of this world, against spiritual wickedness in high places." If we are in conflict with one another, I'm not your enemy. You're not my enemy. Their sin is our enemy – NOT THEM!

A good wife, mother and homemaker. A man wants his wife to take pride in her home and her role as wife and mother. Take care of business at home and stop complaining about your duties. Don't allow him to hide his feelings by becoming a workaholic. It turns into a hiding place for his fear of failure. Prevent him from using his work as an excuse not to live more fully in other areas. It also becomes a place of escape for feelings of aggression as well. Build him up daily, he has a HUGE job! Mother his children with love, compassion and tenderness. He's depending on you to secure a home environment of warmth and growth for his children.

The Heart of the Home

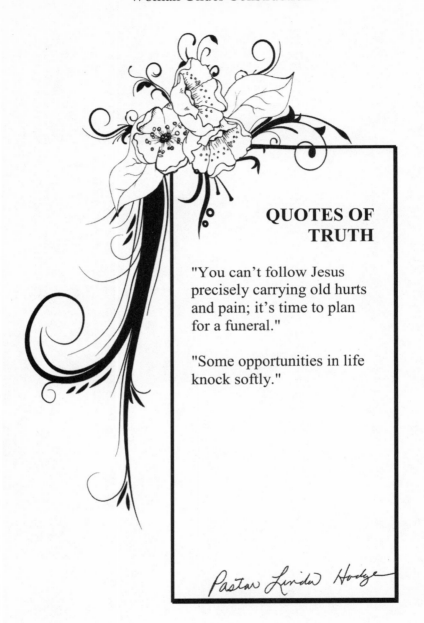

QUOTES OF TRUTH

"You can't follow Jesus precisely carrying old hurts and pain; it's time to plan for a funeral."

"Some opportunities in life knock softly."

Pastor Linda Hodge

Chapter Eleven

Build for Your Future

G od has some new thing in store for you in your life. We know in order to be able to embark upon the new, you have to determine in yourself that, "I'm ready to let go of the past." At times, moving on from past memories is not an easy decision to make. Releasing the old, and embracing the new, brings a rush of emotions to surface. Jesus said, "And no one puts new wine into old wineskins. For the wine would burst the wineskins, and the wine and the skins would both be lost. New wine calls for new wineskins," (Mark 2:22, NLT). *You must shut the door to your past, and allow God to open another door for you.*

I'm sure you have noticed from time to time that while opening a door, to your surprise, the door was harder to open than you had imagined. As a matter of fact, the door looks like every other day in your life. The weight of the door isn't visibly evident to your eyes. But, as you are opening the door, you experience the challenge of the door's heaviness. Nevertheless, you stick with it. You don't change your mind to stop pushing because you know that on the other side of the door is your place of destination. Despite how difficult it is to push open the door, keep pushing with all the power that you can bear. Push until that door opens!

I don't know what is on the other side of the "closed" door in your life you are trying to open. But, I do know it is worth every ounce of fight you can muster up to exert. Some doors require more energy to push open than others. As long as you continually sit down on your broken dreams, constant failures, and shattered hopes, you won't ever make it to the other side of the door.

However, before you can attempt to push open the door, you have to stop feeling sorry for yourself about; the sins, mistakes, and missed opportunities of the past. It's time you forgive yourself. If you have asked for forgiveness, God has thrown it in the sea of forgiveness. There is no more remembrance of it in His mind. Why do you choose to keep your mistakes in the center of your mind?

Some opportunities in life knock softly. The gentle tap can hardly be detected by the heart. Such favorable times in your life are like a ship that glides through the water; after a few minutes, all noticeable residue of the ship's after splash is no longer evident to the naked eye. In other words, there are no traces that the ship was ever there.

> Do not call to mind the former things, or ponder things of the past. Behold, I will do something new, now it will spring forth; will you not be aware of it? I will even make a roadway in the wilderness, rivers in the desert (Isaiah 43:18-19).

This scripture is very simply saying, "Don't you dare let the things of the past play defeated re-runs in your mind. The past is dead; it's time for you to bury it! It's easier said, than done I know.

Oftentimes, the future can be a bit scary. We are accustomed to living life in a very familiar and comforting manner. Getting out of our comfort zone and traveling on a less familiar road can be frightening to say the least. Just think about it. When you travel to work, you normally take the same roads, get on the same freeway, drive into the same parking lot, and park in the same general area. And, you normally repeat that same process upon your return to home.

Our minds are so accustomed to repeats that when we "try" to think of something different, our brain almost has a mind of its own. It wants to think about what makes it feel comfortable. You have to take charge of your thoughts, and "think" about what you are contemplating. Casually, without any hesitation, we allow thoughts of our mind to come and go freely at their own will. Unbridled and unchecked, they are like racing cars – speeding through our minds, trying to be the first one to reach their place of destination.

When we allow our thoughts to go wrong, then our emotions rule our minds. In order to overcome that, you need to learn to rule your emotions with the Word of God, wisdom and rational thinking. Permitting emotional perceptions to rule is like walking a tightrope across a deep chasm without a safety net. The likelihood of catastrophe is high.

Have you ever felt pain from a loss so intense that you thought you suffocate? Perhaps, you experienced one of life's blows that nearly knocked the wind out of you. Its affects were emotionally paralyzing and self-defeating. I'm sure we all have had our share of the "knockdowns and bruises" of life, and some of us are still plowing through the debris of unmet needs, and unresolved issues. *It's time to release those hurts and pains once and for all.* You can't follow Jesus precisely carrying old hurts and pain; it's time to plan for a funeral.

Jesus once responded to a man in a slightly offensive matter. The gentlemen had informed Jesus that he wanted to work with him in his ministry. However, his father expired and he informed Jesus that he had to first go and bury his father. Our Lord said to him, "Follow Me; and allow the dead to bury their own dead" (Matthew 8:22). He was not telling the man to ignore his responsibilities to his parents.

Rather, Jesus was warning him that his desire to hold on to his old life threatened him from following the new life which he had been called.

The Lord has called you to a new life, and to a new and better future. But you risk missing it if you refuse to bury the dead things of your past. If you continue to sit by the graveside, of what "coulda" or "shoulda" been, then you can't build for your future. What are you grieving over today? Your mourning days are over! Dry your eyes, throw away the Kleenex™ box – you won't need it any longer.

You may need to lose some relationships, stop dating certain people or hanging around some sketchy places. The longer you delay detachment, the more you become intertwined in the web of deceit. You may be feeling, "How I can build my life when I have so many open wounds." Emotional wounds that occur as a result from hurts are; rejection, abandonment, abuse, neglect, violence, manipulation, and embarrassment. What are some of the warning signs that indicate you may be plagued by past hurts; when you can't "let go of," when you can't "move on from," and when you can't "get over" the past.

People cannot "let go" of their past, nor should they try. They might be able to "move on," but the pain of the past remains. Telling people to "get over it," only adds more pain. What they really need is freedom from; the hurts; psychological wounds; painful memories; heartbreaks; and other emotional baggage that interferes with enjoying life. From time to time, healing past hurts or emotional wounds typically requires dealing with what the enemy has done.

> And, behold, there was a
> woman which had a spirit of
> infirmity eighteen years, and
> was bowed together, and could
> in no wise lift up herself. And
> when Jesus saw her, he called

her to him, and said unto her,
Woman, thou art loosed from
thine infirmity. And he laid his
hands on her: and immediately
she was made straight, and
glorified God, (Luke 13:11-13).

This story tells of a woman who had been bent double by "a spirit" until Jesus freed her from her bondage. Jesus attributes her bondage to Satan. The account does not indicate that she suffered a physical injury or illness that Jesus healed, or from which he made her well or whole. He freed her from bondage. Such burden had spiritual roots. This passage indicates that the physical appearance came from a spiritual source. Thus, we must realize there are some conditions that are brought on by spiritual forces.

When we recognize that hurts have to do with spiritual sources, we can use spiritual applications to heal the situation. Satan is always looking for an opportunity. Consider 1 Peter 5:8 which states, "Be sober, be vigilant; because your adversary the devil, as a roaring lion, walketh about, seeking whom he may devour." But Jesus came to heal such afflictions. "How God anointed Jesus of Nazareth with the Holy Ghost and with power: who went about doing good, and healing all that were oppressed of the devil; for God was with him," (Acts 10:38).

Your future lies beyond the storms of the present, and you cannot get there by planting a memorial in the past. What kind of life are you constructing for yourself? Are you building your life properly? Are you using the right materials? If you plan to walk in your destiny, you need to be building toward the future all the time. You do this by replacing the wrong thought with the right thought, and you must constantly meditate on the new thought. Joshua 1:8 reminds us:

> This book of the law shall not
> depart out of thy mouth; but
> thou shalt meditate therein day
> and night, that thou mayest
> observe to do according to all
> that is written therein: for then
> thou shalt make thy way
> prosperous, and then thou shalt
> have good success.

I love that Scripture, because it lets me know that my success isn't determined by how many brownie points I get from someone, or how I perform. Rather, as I meditate and, be a doer of the Word, I will automatically have good success. Therefore, my success isn't determined by someone else, but it is solely determined by my obedience, and discipline to the Word of God.

So exactly what are the steps to build my future, especially when I'm hurting?

1. Ask God to heal you from something that's been bothering you.
2. Ask God to reveal to you the past memory that still hurts you.
3. Ask God to remove the pain of those memories and heal you.
4. Understand that God may show up in your memories, especially the destructive ones to bring you security.
5. Recognize that change happens over time.
6. You will recognize when pressure situations arise, but now you respond with Godly wisdom.
7. You will one day turn around and realize that God has transformed your memories.
8. You know you are healed when you do not hide memories, but can share them freely.

Below, I have written a prayer that I want you to read aloud to complete the "Building for Your Future" process:

I renounce hatred, anger, resentment, revenge, retaliation, unforgiveness and bitterness in the name of Jesus. I forgive any person who has ever hurt me?, disappointed me, abandoned me, mistreated me or rejected me in the name of Jesus. I renounce all fear, unbelief, and doubt in the name of Jesus. I renounce all selfishness, self-will, self-pity, self-rejection, self-hatred and self-promotion in the name of Jesus. And, I renounce all ungodly thought patterns and belief systems in the name of Jesus.

Woman of God, I need you to know that God is sifting carefully through the sawdust and scrap piles of the house He is building. God is patiently gathering up all the nails together, whether they are straight or bent, new or used. He is sending out thousands of bricklayers and workers to gather up all the chipped bricks that have been discarded by society. God is repairing you right now – right in front of the devil. You are in the Master's hands. You are reading this book because God is going to use you. Your "hour" was not here yesterday, but your hour has come now! God is ready to glorify your life. The Greek word for "glorify" means, "to put on display." Yes, you used to be bent, but God is straightening you out so He can put you on display. He wants the world to see how He uses ordinary people who became extraordinary in the Master's hand.

[143]

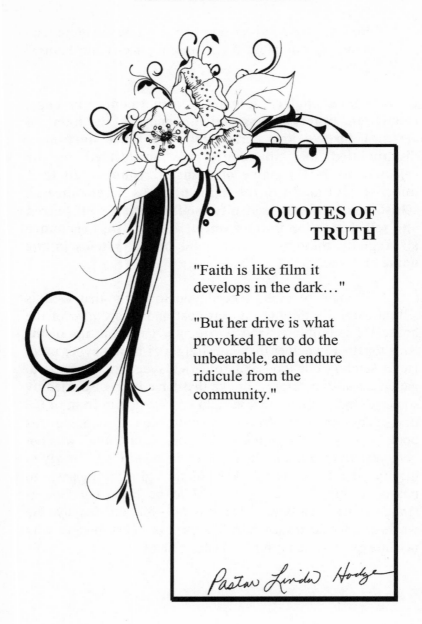

QUOTES OF TRUTH

"Faith is like film it develops in the dark…"

"But her drive is what provoked her to do the unbearable, and endure ridicule from the community."

Pastor Linda Hodge

Chapter Twelve

Before & After Pictures

ictures of before and after a project is completed best
captures the "spirit" of the construction process.
Seeing the construction of a new home has always
been fascinating to my husband and me. As I stated before,
we love watching the transformation method; whether it's a
new home under construction, someone who drastically lost
lots of weight, or a person experiencing a "make-over."

Changing from one state to another state requires
commitment and the ability to remain persistent under
uncomfortable circumstances. Your ability to persevere in
the face of setbacks and disappointments is your measure of
belief in yourself and your ability to succeed. Persistence is
the iron quality of success. The most important unique asset
you have is the characteristic that separates you from
everyone else.

Recently, my husband and I discussed the difference
between an average person and one who excels in their
endeavors. For us, the one word that describes the type of
tenacity that each possesses was "persistence." When you
pursue in the face of inevitable setbacks, delays, and
disappointments, you demonstrate to yourself and to the
people around you that you have the qualities of self-
discipline and self-mastery that are indispensable for the
achievement of any great success.

Thus, in order to have first-rate "before & after"
pictures, you must have unshakable determination and

[145]

persistence. Eventually, you will discover there is nothing in the world that can stop you. Goals will transform into realities. The story of the woman with the issue of blood found in Luke 8:41-49 depicts a woman who had an amazing amount of perseverance. The Scriptures provide the account of what she had to push her way through to receive her miracle. Here is a brief background of biblical times. Women were considered secondary, or second-class citizens, where men looked upon them as "other."

With females considered as having no real identity, that concept changes the fabric of society. The female gender was portrayed as weak-minded and fragile, while men were viewed as courageous, strong, and wise. This woman was considered "contaminated" due to her condition of suffering from a constant menstrual flow. Under normal menstrual cycles, the woman was ritually unclean, and men were urged to separate himself from his wife several days before and after her period to avoid contamination.

Nonetheless, despite how society had "labeled" this woman, she possessed unshakable persistence and chose to go out in the public. She could have chosen to remain in the comfort of her home, praying and hoping to get well. But instead, she put her faith to action by pressing her way into town, where she heard that Jesus was expected to arrive. Making her way through the crowd must have been a tireless and depleting adventure. Crawling on the city streets must have been demeaning to say the least.

However, her drive is what provoked her to do the unbearable, and endure ridicule from the community. Yes, she still forced herself through the annoyed crowd of bystanders. She is definitely a woman of persistence and endurance. In response to her actions, Jesus said to her, *"your faith has made you well."* In First Corinthians 15:58, the Apostle Paul writes: "Therefore, my beloved brethren, be ye steadfast, unmovable, always abounding in the work of the Lord, forasmuch as ye know that your labour is not in vain in the Lord."

In the Eastern part of the world, people plant a tree called the Chinese bamboo. During the first four years, they water and fertilize the plant with seemingly little or no visible results. Then, throughout the fifth year, they again apply water and fertilizer – and in five weeks' time, the tree grows 90 feet. The obvious question is: did the Chinese bamboo tree grow ninety feet in five weeks, or did it grow 90 feet in five years? The answer is simple. The tree grew ninety feet in five years. What's more, if at any time during those five years the people had stopped watering and fertilizing the tree, it would have died.

The irony of this story is if at any time you stop working on your purpose-driven task, quit and give-up on your dream (or life), and then you will stop growing. The "before & after" process takes inner strength. The trait of strength is defined as; power, might, robustness, toughness, fortitude, backbone, and stamina. Scriptural text in Isaiah 52:1-2 gives us an eye-view of how the "before & after" process appears. Take this journey with me:

> Awake, Awake, O Zion, cloth yourself with strength. Put on your garments of splendor, O Jerusalem, the holy city. The uncircumcised and defiled will not enter you again. Shake off your dust; rise up, sit enthroned, O Jerusalem. Free yourself from the chains on your neck, O captive Daughter of Zion.

A great deal transpires in this verse. It is necessary to point out each step of God's process. Let's examine and go deeper. Look closer at this woman and the message that it is transpiring to us. The writer is saying, "Awake, Awake, O

Zion…," suggesting that the writer is extremely serious about sharing his point that he finds it necessary to repeat himself a couple of times. He wants her to awaken from her slumber, and be alerted to her true condition. The words snapped her from the sleep that shrouded her mind, pulling her from the dream in which she was hidden. She was trapped by her past yet afraid of her future, reaching forward, while always looking back.

Traps have a way of holding you hostage; unable to move, and putting you almost in a position of paralysis. Ironically, this is also a hopeful state. Can you imagine, looking around, hearing everything, but still unable to move? I've heard numerous stories where patients who were in a comatose state were aware of everything around them. But, as hard as a patient tried, and although exasperating every ounce of energy, he could not manage to open his eyes or grasp a hand to signal he was at least aware of your presence.

I believe the messenger was saying, "Wake up! It is very late, and you are in danger of remaining captive!" This daughter of Zion was sleepy with oppression and depression. Withdrawn and alone, restrained and weary, she wondered if she would ever be free. Zion could have been depressed because of some "loss" she experienced in her life. But when you really think about it, all of life is a loss. From the day we are born, we begin to lose something. We grow older and lose time. You graduate from preschool or kindergarten and leave behind safe places and special little friends. We make investments and lose money. Unfortunately, we make bad decisions and lose self-confidence.

One of the major skills we must all master in life is the ability to cope with loss. This loss can appear in many forms; loss of a love one, loss of self-esteem, a role, control, financial security, a fantasy relationship. When we fail to adjust to loss, many find themselves oppressed and depressed. I have experienced a series of losses throughout my life. However through the Word of God, my coping skills, and rapid speed to adjust to its absence, I made my way out of the tunnel of despair. We adjust quickly to some losses and hardly notice the passing of a rapid depression. Other losses are not easy to accept, either because they piggyback on top of previous losses or because we feel that the loss was unwarranted.

It's really astonishing how we react when we think that the infliction was unwarranted. I can remember as a young girl, being unjustly spanked (whipped) for a behavior I didn't commit. Of course, you being the child, the parent is always right. There's no recourse but to suffer through the pain without anyone coming to your defense. Sadly, you learn to move-on to the next affliction. What does suffering from depression after experiencing a significant loss feel like? One person said when she woke up in the morning, she was actually afraid to get out of bed. Another said, "I have a sinking feeling, like I'm in a dark hole."

The messenger in the book of Isaiah called her by name. "O Zion." He wanted her to know for certain that he was speaking directly to her. She probably thought that she had been forgotten and forsaken. When you are forgotten that means you are erased from the memory of someone. But being forsaken denotes you are left without support. You don't have anyone to call for an assuring word of encouragement. There is no one to share your heart, secrets, aspirations, hopes or dreams.

Chapter 52 of Isaiah demonstrates how the messenger recognized Zion's weakness and said, "Clothe yourself with strength." He said clothe "yourself." There are certain objects that no other human can provide. She needed inner strength, the type only God supplies. Inner strength is inward fortitude, stamina, persistence. It is the ability to remain calm under pressure. Godly inner strength comes from peace. The Apostle Paul says, "And let the peace of God rule your hearts, (Colossians 3:15). The word "*rule*" from the Greek language was used to portray the umpire or referee who

[149]

judged the athletic games in the ancient world. There is a place whereby the peace of God can begin to call the shots and make all the decisions in your life, instead of fear, regret, and shame.

The secret to renewing your strength is WAITING on the Lord. God's Word in Isaiah 40:31a says, "But they that wait upon the Lord shall renew their strength." At times, you may not have been able to explain it or prove it, but you knew you were waiting on something to happen in your life. The devil said, "You need to give up and die, "but something inside you said, "Hold out a little while longer." The devil said, "You're not going to get it." But something else said, "Wait!" You're hurting, but "Wait." You're crying, but WAIT! You've missed it, but WAIT on the Lord and everything is going to be all right!

Isaiah 40:31b states, "They shall mount up on wings as eagles; they shall run, and not be weary; and they shall walk, and not faint." God declares, "I'll cause your wings to stretch out. You will mount up on wings like eagles. I'll take you above the top of the storm clouds." You see, the eagles do not fly in the storm; they soar above the storm. Spreading their wings wide, eagles use the wind blowing against them to take fly higher instead of lower. Don't allow the wind to bring you down. If you stretch out on God's Word, the same wind that is attempting to take you under will hold you up and carry you over into the glory of God.

You're going to walk and not faint, but first you must come to God with your whole heart. Humble yourself and tell the Lord that you're unable to do it alone. Tell the Lord that you've tried, but you can't seem to get the victory – you can't get up. "Lord, I've been lying here on the grounds of adversity and defeat. Lord, I can't get up." But the Bible says, "The God of all grace will strengthen, perfect and establish you."

Then pointing to clothes that had been stripped from her, the messenger urged, "Put on your garments of splendor." I believe these garments represent her crushed hopes and discarded dreams. The messenger thrust them back into her hands. There are some things that we allow to slip through our hands. Although we thought we had a firm grip on them, they have a way of crumbling right before our eyes. The messenger thrust Zion's belongings back into her hands. I can imagine that she must have marveled how the items had been kept safe and intact. She had feared she would never see them again. Clutching them in her hand she thought, do I dare try this again. I failed when I was younger and stronger. I've been unfaithful and unthankful, are these still mine?

The messenger sensed her fear and kindly reassured her in terms that are more intimate. *"O Jerusalem, the holy city. The uncircumcised and defiled will not enter you again."* Essentially, he told her, "I know who you are, what you have done, and what has happened to you." But *"shake off your dust,"* which signifies an aggressive removal of all that had dirtied or soiled her. The dust is the remains of past journeys and failures. The longer we sit in our past and the more we saturate ourselves in it, the more we are doomed to repeat it. We must shake it off.

The daughter of Zion brushed the dust from her shoulders and arms. She wiped dust from her eyes and tossed it out of her hair. The messenger told her, *"Rise up."* She stood and left her past on the ground. Zion was then told, *"Sit enthroned, O Jerusalem."* She is to no longer sit in her past mistakes, abuses and failures. Romans 8:37 promises believers that life's problems can never, in the end, win: *"No, in all these things we are more than conquerors through him who loved us."* The Bible says that in God we are not simply winners and conquerors, but more than conquerors. Sounds to me like we have ruling authority and accessible power. She was also told a throne had been prepared for her. A position of delegated authority awaits her. Zion is to rest in this position, exercising and enjoying the rights and privileges it provides. And, the last thing he tells her, *"free yourself from the chains on your neck."*

In the natural, the neck is that part of the body that allows you to see in different directions. When the neck is restrained, I have no ability to visualize my God-ordained purpose in life. I can't see past my dilemma or circumstances. You can't achieve what you can't conceive. But, it is my responsibility to unleash myself. I can't be stuck living the re-runs of my life, when a new episode of my life awaits me each and every day.

Many women are so wrapped up in who they think they should be, not who they truly are. They heed to voices from the past that reinforce old ways of thinking and avoid embracing new concepts. Intimidating, nagging voices try to hold them back and make them doubt their courses of action. Distorting, critical voices try to prevent you from seeing circumstances in their present condition. You can't do anything right. You'll never break this habit. Those accusing voices will try to make you live under condemnation.

Isaiah 43:18-19 reminds us, "Do not call to mind the former things, or ponder things of the past. Behold, I will do something new." In other words, don't give it a thought. I'm expecting new opportunities to spring up. It takes courage to drop the old behaviors and embrace new endeavors.

Tribulation becomes the gateway through which God takes us where He wants us to go. He uses trouble as our ticket to promotion. In 2 Corinthians 4:17-18, the scriptures reminds us, "For our light affliction, which is but for a moment, is working for us a far more exceeding and eternal weight of glory." *It's my success and failures that is helping to shape my destiny.* Both have worked as a team to develop you. Most successful women have triumphed not because life has handed them perfection on a silver platter but because they never gave up. They learned to live with their past, flaws, and circumstances, and to succeed nonetheless. I have seen women who have taken the initiative to stop being victims of life's unfortunate situations. These successful women have learned to live their lives without excuses.

My father was a photographer and I remember many times watching him develop film in the dark room. It was always an arduous process for the film to develop and transform from a slight image to a visual picture. Little by little, you would get a clear perspective of what was "transforming." After various solutions were applied to the film itself, it was then hung to dry, so the final process could be completed. How many times have you felt like your life was in developmental stages? Once you thought you had arrived to your life's destination, here comes another hurdle for you to jump. The unexpected challenge left you feeling like you were in a dark place. You weren't able to see a glimpse of light from any direction. Every place you turned for answers or comfort didn't offer any help or reassuring words. No matter how loud you echoed out for help, there was no ear to hear. But, James 1:2 says, "Consider it pure joy, my brothers, whenever you face trails of many kinds, because you know that the testing of your faith develops perseverance.

Faith is like film it develops in the dark…

You may be in a dark place in your life, but your "coach" is here cheering you on to victory. More importantly, The Master Builder, Jesus himself, is interceding for you at the right hand of God. The Holy Spirit is with you, bringing you comfort right now. And God the Father, who knew you before your entry into the world became evidence to your parents, has predestined you for GREATNESS!

As a woman under construction, your "before & after" pictures are becoming clearer and clearer. The construction project appears to be a phenomenal success! Now, lean on the Lord and walk out your purpose.

Bibliography

The Oxford Dictionary, The Oxford Thesaurus: American Edition, Oxford University Press, Inc., 1992

Reader's Digest Medical Encyclopedia, pp. 527-8, 2nd Revised Edition, Readers Digest, 1996

Webster's II New Riverside Dictionary Revised Edition, Houghton Mufflin Company, 1996

Vine, W.E., and Merrill F. Unger, *Vine's Complete Expository Dictionary of Old and New Testament Words*, Thomas Nelson, 1996

Worldwide Sexual Assault Statistics, George Mason University Sexual Assault Services, 2005, SUB I, Room 219 I&M/Fairfax Campus, 4400 University Dr. MS 2B2, Fairfax, VA 22030, www.sexualassaultservices.gmu.edu

The World Bank, www.worldbank.org

Facts and Figures: Sexual Violence in Non-Conflict Situations, United Nations Development Fund for Women, www.unifem.org/campaigns/november25/facts_figures_3.php

Sexual Violence Facts, The World Health Organization, www.who.int/violence_injury_prevention

Stop Violence against Women: Prevalence of Sexual Assault, United Nations Development Fund for Women, www.stopvaw.org/PrevalenceSexualAssault.html or www.unifem.org

National Center for Victims of Crime (2004) www.ncvc.org

Global perspectives on Sexual Abuse, National Sexual Violence Resource Center (NSVRC) www.nsvrc.org

[154]

About The Author

Linda G. Hodge is a wife, mother, grandmother, pastor, motivational speaker, and now she adds the title of author. For more than a decade, Linda has produced conferences, seminars, and extreme makeovers designed to uplift, support and empower women with the tools to renovate and restore their God-given purpose in life. Her commitment to abused women and children is unwavering. By popular demand, and encouragement, Linda was inspired to write her self-help manual, ***Woman Under Construction*** to help bring more women to a place of healing and success.

Linda G. Hodge co-pastors Living Praise Christian Center with her husband, Dr. Fred L. Hodge, Jr. in Chatsworth and Lancaster, California. They have five children and six grandchildren.